Yuletide Bargains
and Other Flawed Choices

WITCHES OF WILLOWMERE BOOK 2

Lorin Petrazilka

FATEBOUND
✦BOOKS
A WOMEN-OWNED IMPRINT

Yuletide Bargains and Other Flawed Choices
First Edition
Copyright 2025 Lorin Z Pillai

All Rights Reserved. Printed in the United States of America.

Published by Fatebound Books
For rights inquires, please contact rights@fateboundbooks.com

FATEBOUND✣BOOKS

ISBN 979-8-9920575-3-9
Cover design by Lorin Z Pillai

For anyone who's ever faced winter armed with pastries,
questionable planning,
and a generous helping of magic.

Table of Contents

Pronunication Guide..1

Chapter 1...3

Chapter 2...15

Chapter 3...21

Chapter 4...27

Chapter 5...33

Chapter 6...41

Chapter 7...51

Chapter 8...59

Chapter 9...65

Chapter 10...73

Chapter 11...83

Chapter 12...95

Chapter 13...103

Chapter 14...111

Acknowledgments...119

About the Author...121

Pronunciation Guide

Briar Whittaker - BRY-ar WIT-tack-er

Silas Thorne - SY-lus THORN

Tabitha - TA-bih-thah

Lughnasadh - LOO-nass-AH

Willowmere - WILL-oh-meer

Hollow Forest - HALL-oh FOR-est

Mirlah - MEER-lah

Sawyer - SOY-yer

Maeve- MAYV

Casimir - CAZ-ih-meer

Chapter 1

In the quaint town of Willowmere, two things were certain as Yule approached: Briar Whittaker would be buried under orders for her legendary Yule Log cakes, and an icy blast from the heart of Hollow Forest would roll in like clockwork to announce the season. Every year the same sudden storm swept through, bringing with it a sparkling, wintry landscape that belonged on postcards. Though the village would be coated in an otherworldly crystalline frost, the 'regulars' of the town always described it simply as "colder than a witch's titty" rather than noting its beauty. The witches of Willowmere, like Briar and her cousin Tabitha, would smile and shake their heads, letting the comment pass. They weren't about to break it to the non-magical locals that the town didn't only seem to have witchy charm, half of its residents were actual witches. And for the record, Briar's boyfriend, the half-Fae moody forest guardian and local lumberjack Silas Thorne, could personally confirm there was *nothing cold* about her particular anatomy.

The thought made her grin as she waved a hand over her

worktable. Measuring cups and spoons began their usual enchanted dance as she directed them. Flour sifted, eggs cracked, sugar shimmered midair. Her kitchen hummed with life, warmth, and the exact right amount of chaos.

Five batches of Yule Log cakes mixed themselves simultaneously, and that was only round one. Deadlines in Willowmere weren't measured in days or hours, this one was set by the coming storm. Once that first frost hit, every witch, human, and vaguely magical woodland creature would be lined up outside Briar's shop demanding her enchanted Yule cakes. Okay, maybe the magical creatures and spirits kept to Hollow Forest, but they always craved her delectable creations, too. Plus, Yule was in two days, so ultimately whether or not the storm came on the day of or before, the cakes had to all be done by the morning of Yule Eve.

Each year she made them a little differently. Last year's crowd favorite had released a spectral burst of snowflakes into the air when sliced. This year's? A forest scene that grew sugared mushrooms before transforming into a glittering Yule village. She had perfected her spell of growing sugar crystals to look like ice. Eat your heart out, Martha Stewart.

Her hands swished again, guiding the batter-filled pans into the ovens. The smell of vanilla, cinnamon, and nutmeg swirled through the air, wrapping her shop in cozy warmth. With twenty minutes to spare before opening, Briar brushed her hands off on her apron and carried two mugs of coffee and a small plate of Joyful Gingerbread Cookies to the table by the window.

Silas was already there, sitting in his favorite spot by the window, gazing out at the edge of Hollow Forest. Normally he'd have made at least three snarky remarks by now. Today, though, he was quiet. Brooding. Which for him wasn't exactly new, but this time it felt heavier somehow. They had gotten into the shop extra early so she could start her cake orders on top of her usual offerings, but this seemed like something other than a begrudging early rousting.

"You seem distracted," she said, sliding into the chair across from him. "You okay?"

He didn't look away from the trees. "Oh, yeah, I'm *great*. Just admiring the way the last leaves flee the coming persecution of winter."

"Wow. Someone's in a mood. I'm hearing shades of Silas "Crabass" Thorne."

He cracked a small smile. "Good ol' dark and broody forest weirdo. It's my thing."

"Mmhmm," she agreed after swallowing a sip of coffee. "Been your thing since the day I met you, stomping through Hollow Forest like a moose with emotional issues."

That earned her a laugh, but the crease between his brows stayed put. And she had to admit, she was a little dismayed, she had thought they'd grown past the gruff mask he had historically donned in order to push people away.

After a moment, he sighed and turned toward her. "Sorry. I got caught up thinking about things. This time of year... it's

5

complicated for me, I guess. I know you love Yule, but for me it's a reminder of some stuff."

She didn't need him to spell it out. He rarely talked about his upbringing in Faerie, and even less about his Fae mother and human father. From what little Briar knew, she made the Wicked Stepmother archetype look like a life coach, and who knew where his dad even was anymore. With Silas being a half-Fae, with one foot out of Faerie and the other in his father's hometown of Willowmere, it made finding his place in the world a challenge.

"Gotta love unrealistic parental demands," she said with a wink.

He huffed a laugh. "You have no idea."

Silas reached for a gingerbread cookie, his faint smile tugging his lips as his fingers brushed hers. He hadn't even taken a bite yet, and she could already feel the spellwork humming between them, the Joyful Gingerbread living up to its name.

Briar smiled in triumph. Her magic had come a long way since she'd opened Bun Intended two years ago. Her pastries carried spells from the moment someone touched them, all the way through the last crumb. Courage Croissants, Muse Muffins, Desire Danishes. Each one crafted with intention, spices, and secret incantations. Being both a kitchen witch and a green witch meant her spells offered a warm, magical push from the baking process *and* the spices she seasoned them with.

The cookie was a small respite against whatever mood had creeped into her cranky-pants boyfriend. Still, as she watched Silas stare out the window again, something in her chest tightened.

The storm hadn't even arrived yet. So why did it already feel like something was coming?

Tabitha's black electric car zoomed by the shop window, the huge gray-and-gold vinyl roses on its hood blurred as it disappeared out of view. Briar and Silas snapped their eyes to each other, the sound of her tires squealing into the parking spot around the corner told them enough. Tabitha was about to rush through the door in a frenzy, late as usual. Moments later they heard hurried clacking of her pointy-toed boots rushing down the sidewalk to get to the shop.

"Made it!" Tabby announced as the door banged shut behind her.

Briar twisted in her seat to face her cousin, two years Briar's junior and only sometimes a functioning adult. However, Briar didn't miss how the twenty-seven-year-old's makeup was beyond perfect, likely with the help of a glamour spell. "You do know what time you said you'd be here, yes? And what time it actually is now?" She lifted a wrist out of habit, then blinked at the bare skin where her watch should have been.

Tabby's eyes tracked the motion. "If you say a hair past a freckle, I swear to Hecate I'm going to cast against you, I'll hex you so pretty you'll thank me," Tabby threatened, lifting her pointer finger.

Silas snorted."You know that's not possible, right?"

Briar smiled, then laughed. The comment could have meant

one of two things, either he was once again insinuating their witchcraft was silly and not real, or he was saying she was already too pretty to improve upon. Given that he had already recanted his years of asserting the former was the case, that magic wasn't real and he only believed in "real shit" as he had long ago claimed, she decided he implied the latter. He had, after all, spent a good amount of time the night before worshipping her body and proclaiming her the most beautiful in all the land. How decidedly Evil Queen of him.

Briar grinned at Tabby. "Well come and give me a hug, I haven't seen you in days!"

Tabitha pulled her too-cute-to-get-dirty apron out of her bag, cinching it around her waist. "And get flour on myself already?" She walked over to Briar, leaned over and pecked her cheek. "I missed you, too. And hello to you, Silas."

Silas twitched half a smile and nodded. They weren't exactly on bad terms, but Tabby hadn't entirely adjusted to the part where Briar's "sworn forest nemesis" had been reclassified to boyfriend. The paperwork, apparently, was still pending.

Tabby brushed past him, not worrying about his lack of greeting as she got to work in her usual way, posting up behind the counter, preparing for customers to come in. She did her common spells before the day started, blessing the counter and the till with abundance and good fortune. Putting bay leaves in the cash drawer to encourage prosperity and whispering incantations for a fruitful day at Bun Intended, Tabitha came to life when she flexed her gray witch skills. Though TabbyTrix, as the knitting circle called her, had her prankster ways and her occasional inability to treat an average day like a normal adult, she truly loved Briar and wanted her success in every way. Tabby put real intention into the magic she added to the store. No tricks, not even a fun spell to make the sugar packets evade the patrons before they could get them into their coffee.

Silas stood from his spot at the window, then headed to the back hall to grab his jacket, satchel which he never went anywhere without, and scarf. The early morning at the shop was his time to help Briar, but with the arrival of Tabby, and the sassy wind that blew in with her, he prepared to make his exit. The women would have their time together, share tea and cookies later when they got a break, and gossip out of earshot. Probably about him. Briar smiled at the thought as she watched him walk. That cantankerous man sure did funny things to her mind. She had to resist the urge to catcall something cringey, like "I hate to see you leave but love to watch you walk away." Rolling her lips as she hid her grin, she instead turned back to her coffee, watching the steam curl out of it as the cold morning frosted the window next to her.

Thoughts on how she was going to fit cake making into the schedule that day took over her attention, because once the customers came in, she'd be busily filling their daily orders. Today and part of tomorrow were probably all she would have left, time-wise. So she'd have to make the effort during the day. Peeling herself away to frost and decorate would probably be difficult, but she had standing plans with Silas after the shop closed. There was no way she'd stay late to bake when she had *him* waiting for her. Briar loved plans, especially plans that included her toes curling. Her cheeks turned nearly as red as the fondant buttons on the gingerbread cookies. She was so lost in thought, she didn't notice Silas sidle up to her. Years spent as the forest creeper gave him some skills in that department.

Silas moving into position was enough of a sign to Tabby for her to head into the kitchen, since he was clearly ready to angle in and steal a kiss from Briar. Peeping their goodbye smooch was not on her schedule.

He smelled of crackling fires after a brisk walk through frost covered woods as he leaned in, Briar had to hold herself back from swooning. The combination of Silas's sexy scent magic *and* his looks did make him rather swoon-worthy. He had a way of sweeping her up with his Fae magic, it unfurled anytime he was close to her. Pulling Briar in close like there was no one else nearby, he tilted his head close to hers. And since Tabby got the hint, no one was there to see just how close he was, narrowing the distance between their hips. With his one hand scooped in around her waist and the other cradling her neck, he used his thumb along her jaw to turn her face up to his. "After the shop closes, you're *mine*," he said, his tone husky. "We have unfinished business from last night."

Closing her eyes as his magical smell enveloped her, she resisted the urge to groan and hike up her leg. That would have most definitely not have been modest shopkeeper behavior. It would have populated under the Naughty Baker heading. Maybe it could be blamed on her Desire Danishes, those deliciously spelled pastries had certainly gotten them into trouble before. But this time they hadn't eaten any, and if they had … well they would have likely already shifted from vertical to horizontal. "Unfinished business? Hmm, I seem to remember a few instances that would prove otherwise."

A lazy smile pulled his mouth to one side. "That doesn't mean that I've had enough of you. I don't think I ever will."

She lowered her eyelashes and smiled, which made his scent stronger. She loved how it would change, how the seasons affected what images the magic would evoke. The smell of a rich fire and warm hearth gave her thoughts of a bear rug, and her naked upon it. He may have acted like a cranky forest creature sometimes, but fortunately his smells were not of the hibernating beast sort. The brief thought almost made her laugh, but before she could he averted the tangent by finally kissing her. His lips capturing hers made the rest of the world melt away.

Snowflakes dusted her skin, sending a delighted shiver up her spine as he pulled away. Releasing a breath, she smiled again, which he returned, but something about it felt a little off. She noticed he even had some ice crystals form on his face, but they quickly vanished.

His magic had somehow grown stronger as winter approached. As she thought about it, she realized she had never *felt* his magic before, not like that. The feelings the magical scents brought out had always been strong, but she never had sensations on her skin or seen any visible signs. The look on his face told her enough, he wasn't happy about how his aptitude grew without his permission. He had always sidestepped his power, pretending for years that magic didn't even exist. The truth was he had his skills regardless of how he felt about them, but being a naysayer was easier for him than facing the fact that he had received unwanted gifts from his mother.

"I'll see you later," he said, clearly avoiding any comments about his escalating magical prowess. Typical.

"My place?" she asked, letting her recognition of his newfound Skin Tickle Snowflake skill lie unmentioned, in spite of the fact that she had already named it. How magnanimous of her to not bring it up.

He nodded. "Tabby will take you home, right? No walking through Hollow Forest at night alone. It gets dark early this close to Yule."

Briar almost giggled, even though it was no laughing matter. Hollow Forest was a hotbed for paranormal activity, all kinds of different spirits and mystical creatures roamed there, as well as the elusive gateway into Faerie that Silas loved to avoid, somewhere deep in the forest. The forest did have a particularly useful shortcut through the bottom tip of it, which shaved twenty minutes off of Briar's bike ride to and from work, but Silas was the only one resilient enough to handle the restless spirits with ease when the sun went down. It had been Briar's half-baked idea to enter the forest unguided in the dark, *twice*, which resulted in events that unfolded with her and Silas's eventual coupling earlier in the year, during harvest season. So, it wasn't *all* bad things that happened in the forest. Still, she wasn't about to tempt fate again. But … she couldn't help considering it.

He eyed her with a suspicious quirk to his eyebrow. "I mean it, Briar. It's too close to Yule to go in there. I want to make sure you're safe. Tabby!" He turned toward the kitchen, waiting for Briar's cousin to appear.

Tabitha poked her head out of the kitchen archway. "Quit bellowing, you moose. I can hear you." The rest of her body followed a moment later, then she walked toward the end of the counter nearest them.

His eyes snapped back to Briar, who cringed and laughed. She knew *exactly* what he was thinking, it had been maybe fifteen minutes since she called him a moose before Tabby even arrived. "It is a fair comparison." She shrugged, then realized what his next thought might be. "I swear neither of us have said that about you before."

"Speak for yourself!" Tabby exclaimed as she leaned against the counter edge. "I've been calling you a moose, at least to myself, for eons."

Staring at Tabby for a moment, he finally laughed. "I knew the Fae were long-lived, but I had no idea that witches were, too. Moose it is, they're majestic after all. And they plow through difficult situations with vigor."

13

Tabitha looked at her nails. "They plow their girlfriends the same way, too."

It was a good thing Briar had just finished taking a sip of coffee, because she would have spit it out if she hadn't swallowed yet. "Tabby!"

TabbyTrix grinned, all too pleased with herself that she had taken every opportunity to skewer Silas. She lifted her hands. "All right, all right. Sorry, just an inappropriate joke. Anyway, yes, Silas, I know you want to make sure I'll drop Briar off when we're done for the day. No shenanigans in the Hollow Forest on the way home."

Silas chuckled at Tabby and shook his head. "Okay, good." He leaned over and kissed Briar once more, not caring that Tabitha didn't have a chance to scoot back to the ovens again.

And with that, Silas breezed out of the shop, the scent of pine and woodsmoke lingering where he'd stood. Maybe he was off to scowl at squirrels, maybe to find the perfect Yule surprise for Briar. Either way, Briar felt the chill he left behind far too quickly.

Chapter 2

The morning blurred into its usual whirlwind—orders popping off, a steady stream of patrons elbowing in for the best pastries, and barely a breath in between. Briar managed only a handful of half-conversations with Tabby, each one swallowed by the next wave of customers.

And just when the shop finally started to quiet... in swept the entire knitting circle. Naturally. They were like the cozy-witch version of a flash mob as they all crowded into the bakery. Their standing order of spell-laced cookies awaited; treats that let them gossip at full cackle volume while keeping their tea-time scandals blissfully private.

All seven of them loved their late mornings spent at Bun Intended. The knitting circle was a code name to make it easier for them to have their usual meets, they were after all the most connected and powerful witch coven in Willowmere. Since Briar's mother, Persephone, and Tabby's mother, Selene, had previously been a part of their coven, the elders often included the two younger witches in their mothers' stead. With both of them crossed over to the summerland, their loss meant not only did the girls not have them for all the various life events and celebrations throughout the years, but the knitting circle no longer had two of their dearly loved sisters of the circle. The reality that Briar and Tabby had to go on with the Wheel of the Year without them was a hardship they leaned on each other for, and also sometimes preferred not to think about. It was sometimes easier to not dwell on the fact that they did not have their moms to talk to on a regular basis, to be there for the highs and lows of life, but also for something as simple as a hug. However, with Tabitha's skills as a hedge witch, they were able to periodically see them in the meeting place between worlds, in the shadow realm. But with them having recently visited for Samhain, they likely weren't going to get to see them until Imbolc in February.

Donna, who generally took charge in most situations, must have caught Briar's facial expression, because she scooped her up in a warm hug. Before Briar knew it the other six of them: Josefine, Agnes, Abigail, Anne, Bronwyn, and Iris, all crowded around and added themselves to it. Someone grabbed Tabby and squished her into the circle as well, making sure both girls got their dose of witchy auntie love.

Briar let out a sigh as the old biddies all released the hug, then gathered around their favorite table. In spite of the reminder of her mother, she loved their daily visit. Their poking and prodding about her love life? Not so much. They had at least chilled out with their comments on their witchy review site, where the previous summary of her shop included more about her romantic prospects than her pastries.

Their chittering over cookies was like a melody of comfortable nonsense. And with the ladies settled in, she and Tabby could finally take a break together. Briar grabbed their usual white-and-yellow teapot that they reserved especially for their tea break together.

"Oh wait!" Tabby said. "Don't put the hot water in yet." She rushed out the front door, presumably to her car. Appearing a few minutes later with a large, crinkled paperbag, she motioned for Briar to sit down. "Here! The first gift of Yule."

"You beat me to it!" Briar exclaimed. It wasn't even Yule yet, and Tabby had already fired the first shot in their annual gift-giving duel. Briar considered lodging a formal protest, but she loved presents far too much to risk discouraging her. She was a self self-proclaimed gift slut, though until Silas, her only spicy encounters involved cinnamon and nutmeg. Really she loved the whole idea of gifting, from start to finish, from coming up with ideas, to either buying or making something, getting creative with wrapping, and even the presentation of it. Aside from loving the decorations of Yule, she loved the spirit of gift-giving.

"Well open it!" Tabby demanded. "It'll make sense why in a moment."

Briar squealed with glee, but then remembered TabbyTrix's nature. "Wait, is this a prank gift? This isn't like the cheese printer, is it?"

Tabitha cackled, looking like she was reliving the funniest joke ever. "Ahhh that was a good one, but no, *not* a cheese printer."

Briar narrowed her eyes. Tabby had fully invested herself in the performance when Briar unwrapped the 'cheese printer,' the box promising all kinds of crazy claims, saying it could print a picture on any kind of sliced cheese. It even had a melted, distorted portrait of a mother and baby on it. "Who would want this?" Briar had asked when she received it the Yule prior. "Who wouldn't?" Tabby had responded with so much conviction Briar shrugged and eventually muttered something about being able to use it in the shop. When she opened the so-called printer? Yeah, no printer inside. It was a beautiful scarf instead, a shade of moss green that made Briar's auburn reddish hair pop, and was utterly perfect for Briar. Leave it to Tabby to throw in a trick, even on Yule. Ultimately it hadn't been a prank, but the misdirection caused a moment of confusion that Tabby had found absolutely hilarious. And wow had she leaned into her acting skills, she completely sold the idea of a cheese printer before Briar finally opened the box. So much so, Briar almost wondered if at that point she then wanted the preposterous and not at all real printer.

TabbyTrix was *still laughing* about it as Briar started opening the bag, which could barely be defined as a gift bag, then pulled out a breathtaking porcelain teapot. The delicate pine cone, evergreen bough, and holly details on the pristine glazed white were beyond perfect, and a thin gold band ran around it that was so bright it had to be real gold. "Tabby, it's so beautiful, I love it. Thank you."

"I decided you needed more Yule-inspired things around. That's not all." Tabitha pointed with her chin for Briar to look further into the bag.

Long strands of sparkling snowflake garlands were coiled in the bottom. Briar smiled, typical that Tabby had chaotically wrapped her gift using the second part of the present as mediocre padding. It may have been subpar in terms of softness, but it was a top tier garland. She could forgive it not being a good cushion for the teapot based on how pretty it was. And fortunately the teapot had fared well during transport, in spite of Tabby's insane driving habits.

"I love it! Let's put it up!" Briar said as she admired it.

"Tea first! Then we can decorate. Plus I don't especially want to brush my butt along Donna's arm, she is right next to the main window. Maybe after the knitting circle is done with their hen house session."

Briar laughed. "Agreed."

They enjoyed their tea and a few of the extra cookies from the knitting circle's order, and chatted until the next set of customers came in. They decorated in between orders, getting iridescent glitter on each other as they hung the sparkle-encrusted garlands. Briar had already put up bundles of pine boughs in the corners of each window and the door the day before, so the strands added the finishing touch to what would eventually match the wintry landscape out of the windows. Nothing like a little visual magic to go with actual magic.

Everything felt so blissfully ordinary, baking, banter, and Tabby belting witchy Yuletide carols. Still, something tugged at Briar, whispering that the calm wouldn't last. Probably nothing. Just a hint of existential dread and an otherworldly storm gathering in the middle of a haunted forest. Totally fine.

Chapter 3

It felt more like Samhain than Yule, given Tabby was driving like she had a demon on her tail. For some reason Briar had not counted on the imminent death portion of the journey for the drive back to her house. How silly of her.

"Hex, Tabby!"

"My bad! This damn lead foot." Tabby stomped the floorboard for emphasis, nearly making Briar swallow her tongue, then gave her a deadpan as they screeched to a stop sign.

"Three seconds," Briar said. "You have to wait three seconds at a stop before you gas it."

"It's an electric car, babe. There is no gas to wait on."

"Don't be cute. Stop launching us forward like you're late to an orgy."

"I'm late for a date. A very hot one."

"Fantastic. Slow down anyway."

"Fineee. Even though this intersection is emptier than a vampire's pulse."

"Maybe so. But traffic laws exist."

"Ugh. Goody-two-boots strikes again." Tabby wilted into an opera-level sigh. Drama. Pure drama.

They arrived miraculously alive at Briar's two-bedroom grovestone cottage on the east side of town. The tip of Hollow Forest jutted down from the north side, and separated most of Willowmere from the East End, which consisted only of a narrow strip of quaint houses. They offered more garden space, but were farther from the village center.

Tabby waited a few minutes with the car running. With her headlights shining on the unlit house so Briar could make her way up the stairs, she headed out once Briar had unlocked her door and waved her off. Tabby had that hot date to scootch off to, after all.

Having a magical lock no one else could pick gave Briar peace of mind that not a soul had breached the perimeter of the house. But something settled strangely, there was a pensive quality to the air. Like the nearby trees were holding their breath. Which of course was not ominous in the least.

Briar pushed the door open after the unlocking spell decided she had fumbled it enough times to open. Darkness squatted inside the house, quiet and patient, waiting for her to fill the space.

Her house always seemed to sigh when she walked in, like it was relieved she came home. It was always happier when she was there, swirling spices into meals in the kitchen or tending the garden out back. But with the early darkness and winter threatening to begin at every turn, the garden had been put to sleep after the last harvest.

Asking the lights to turn on with a swish of her hands, flicking on the oven to preheat it, then lighting a few candles on the counter, the place sparked to life and became a haven of cozy comfort. With the casserole she had prepared the day before now baking and a little time to spare before Silas would arrive at 7:30 p.m., she decided to take a shower.

Heat from the uneaten casserole had diminished to barely-there warmth as the cuckoo clock ticked past 8:25. He was *never* late. He was good about being punctual, and he knew Briar being the planner she was, tardiness got under her skin quickly. She had thought about calling him ten minutes prior, but kept telling herself to be patient and that he was probably moments from bounding up the porch stairs.

"Fuck it, I'm calling him." The line rang and rang. Briar frowned, it wasn't like she was surprised, he never turned his ringer on anyway. Not even on vibrate. What a shame, most girls know the value of a good vibrate setting on any device. But Silas was practically old fashioned with his ways, nearly having an aversion to technology. She wondered why he even bothered having a phone. "So I can look at pictures of you when we aren't together" he had said once. Yeah, that comment made her turn into putty. But what had really sent her swooning was that he wasn't trying to be sweet, that was simply the truth. He didn't take or make calls, he liked pictures. His phone had been filled with photos of inanimate objects before Briar. Tree stumps, fallen logs with moss on them, close-ups of bark. Typical lumberjack core. Now it was chock full of memories of the two of them. She thought they'd be making more memories that evening. It was meant to be the small reprieve from the busy day of baking as Yule prepared to descend with icy grandeur.

Clicking her nails on the counter, the clock ticked in time to her tapping. It struck 8:30, and the midhour cuckoo made an appearance. Briar held her breath as the carved raven cawed from the tiny door above the clock face. Something was wrong. She could feel it. This wasn't wrong in a "I forgot my buns in the oven" kind of way. This was a horror movie zoom lens wrongness. A cockeyed camera tilt showing the pinecone weights and the oak leaf pendulum swinging from the bottom of the clock, as the cawing marked the half-hour. It was the dawning of realization that something that didn't fit into the human world had edged its way in.

Briar straightened and sucked in a breath. She needed to find him, and fast. Mentally sifting through the next steps she could take, Briar decided she needed to eat something. If she was going out into the dark night alone, she needed to make sure she had some sustenance first. Briar could picture herself in a full hangry tirade when she eventually found Silas if she didn't eat anything. Then she'd be the one ready to stomp through the forest.

Within moments she had a scoop of casserole on a plate, which she started wolfing down while planning her next move. Water. She'd need water. Briar had wandered for hours in Hollow Forest without it and had learned her lesson. Since Silas didn't live inside the forest, she shouldn't need to plan to go in, however she'd need to be prepared for heading to his place and back on foot. It was too late for her bike, with not enough streetlights and part of the pathway there being overly bumpy cobblestones, hoofing it would be better. Jacket. Scarf. Hat. Phone, which had a flashlight that would come in handy. No. She needed to bring an *extra* flashlight that was an actual flashlight, not depending solely on a phone battery tonight.

Finishing her quick meal, she left the plate where it was and didn't bother covering the pan before jamming it into the fridge, fully aware her future self would judge her life choices. Present Briar had a crisis to manage. She grabbed her essentials, swung on her coat, and stepped outside.

Silas Thorne was missing, and she would find him. Then she'd give him the kind of scolding only a girlfriend who cared way too much could deliver: equal parts fury, relief, and inappropriate levels of kissing.

Chapter 4

Ominous was a word she wished didn't describe this evening. But unfortunately, it was the perfect descriptor. Silas's house was dark and empty. And it didn't help that the Hollow Forest towered practically overheard. Saying he didn't live in the forest was a generous way to put it. The house wasn't *in* the woods, but move one foot west, and yep, you're in there. Swallowed by the dark, gnarled oaks.

Standing in the driveway in front of the log cabin, she spun, looking around for any nearby rustling bushes or some other announcement of his arrival. He was late to surprise her and tell her it was all a plan to get her to come there. Goodbye false hope. Hello creepy woods, and being alone right next to them.

A slow breath through the nose was the perfect fix for this tense and unsettling situation. Yep, totally effective at convincing Briar that there wasn't a malevolent entity that barely evaded her flashlight every time she shined it into the treeline. Imagining the Hidebehind or some other strange cryptid wasn't helping, neither was the memory of the dark spirits that chased her down in the forest on Lughnasadh. One of those entities had taken the form of Tabitha, and was so convincing that it almost managed to catch Briar. The fact that entities can't speak was the first clue that something was amiss. She had to remind herself of that night, because if she suddenly did see Silas pop out of the trees, it wasn't guaranteed to actually be him.

Briar took another steadying breath. She needed to keep her focus on the fact that Silas was apparently missing, and there was no sign of where he might have gone. Decision time then, she needed to figure out her next move, or find a clue. She walked up the steps to the creaking wood porch, then looked in the windows. Nothing. Not even a hint that he'd been there. *Wait.* There was a chair knocked over, and his satchel was hanging on the chair by the table. He had it with him at the shop and left with it. He *had* been there. She looked for other hints as to where he had gone, when she caught a glimmer out of the corner of her eye.

Near the top of his front door something gleamed with a strange, cold aura. She took a step toward it and gasped when she realized what it was.

An arrow. Shot into his front door, right at what would have been Silas's eye line. Ice crystals formed around where it had penetrated, like the arrow was sent straight from the bitter arctic. Something coiled around the shaft which looked like it had a coating of frost. The fletching seemed intricate, not like a regular arrow at all.

The thought of what a regular arrow might look like made her scoff, it wasn't like she knew anything about arrows or archery. But there was something different about this. It didn't look like what she would expect an arrow to look like. There were fine carvings on it, strange markings. Letters that she didn't recognize. Briar reached up to feel what was around the shaft, only to discover it was some kind of paper. Uncoiling it, she yanked her hand back at the biting cold of it. Briar squinted her eyes, taking a closer look at it.

"Oh hex, it's some kind of messenger arrow." That was a thing, right? At least she knew it used to be. Standing up on her tiptoes, she unrolled it in quick, careful flicks to avoid touching it, to try and read it without knocking it out of position. Getting it open without disturbing the arrow from where it was lodged in the door, she discovered the words were illegible. The letters it was written with were like the carvings, unfamiliar and ornate.

Dread settled in her stomach and the blood drained from her face.

This arrow was made by the Fae.

She had never seen their writing before, or seen their handiwork, but that carving was some Rivendell elf shit if she ever saw it. Silas had left his satchel, and that man never went anywhere without his murse. That meant he probably left in a hurry or maybe even against his will. She knew he didn't want to return to Faerie, and an arrow in the door didn't exactly say "gentle request" to her.

Testing the door to see if it was locked, she found it swung open easily. Also not the best sign that the door was left unsecured.

Stepping inside like the ghosts from the forest might have made their way in, she grabbed the bag from where it hung on the chair, slung it across her body, then headed back out.

She didn't know what it meant, but she knew she needed help. "Ugh, Tabby's on a date. I can't call her." Tapping her foot on the wooden boards, she made up her mind. Silas was *missing*. And no one, not Silas, not Tabby, would want Briar to go into Hollow Forest alone ... again. Because that's what Briar was two seconds from doing. She was ready to charge in there, find the portal, then bring him home. Fae be damned. Briar resolved to call Tabby and ask for help. As a gray witch, and a talented one at that, nobody was better at finding weird doorways into other realms or liminal spaces. Tabitha Whittaker was the reigning witch at getting into places she shouldn't be. Briar didn't think she had ever crossed the boundary into Faerie, but it was the perfect time to try.

Glancing at her phone, the time read 9:15. If the date didn't go well, it was probably already over. But if it did ... she might be interrupting. Briar debated calling, then thought about texting. She abandoned both ideas, and decided to go with the Witch Phone. That was the name she had come up with after she learned the threading spell, which is a gray witch skill some have that allows one witch to connect to another or multiples using a magical thread. Quick messages can be sent, and the thread can be pulled taut to draw a witch toward the caller. Pretty handy and at least mildly invasive. Maybe a lot invasive depending on what state Tabby was in. If it was a state of duress because the date was a disaster, maybe

30

the call would be welcome. But if she was in a state of *undress*, well that would be a more uncomfortable situation. Wherever Tabby was and whatever she was doing, she was about to get yoinked to Briar's side. Hopefully she'd be cool with it.

Wind picked up as Briar closed her eyes, swirling her hair as she tunneled within herself and focused her intention. Inhaling a long, slow breath through her nose, she pictured Tabby, saw the thread form, saw the line connect across the distance, then held her breath and pulled the thread. "Tabby, I need you."

Tabitha's gaze locked with Briar's across that divide, seeing each other in their minds' eyes. "I hear you. I'm coming."

Chapter 5

The rift opened right next to Briar, a smoky gray slice through the air that grew vertically. A heeled boot stepped through first, followed by the rest of Tabitha. She had hedge-ridden from wherever she was straight to Briar's side. What an icon.

"Bitch, this better be good! Also hi, are you okay?"

Briar nodded, hugged her, then motioned with her chin to the arrow. "Check it out. We've had a visitor, and they've taken something important."

Tabby's eyes flashed to the arrow. She dropped her arms from Briar's shoulders to look at it. "Hex, it's Fae."

"Yep. Can you read it?"

"No, I don't know anyone who can. Aside from Silas."

"Yeah, he won't be able to translate, until we rescue him I imagine. I think they've taken him. He was an hour late for our date, so I came here. His satchel was inside," she said, motioning to the bag she now wore. "That was my first clue, I mean aside from not showing up, because he's never late. But he doesn't go anywhere without his bag." She ran her hand over the tooled leather strap. Briar had gifted the bag to him when they celebrated Mabon. They'd been dating less than two months, which was definitely the "maybe a nice card" phase, not the "deeply personal handcrafted accessory" phase. But Briar had walked past the leatherworker's shop, seen that tall, rectangular crossbody beauty, and basically blacked out.

Every piece there was one-of-a-kind. If she didn't buy it, some other stylish woodland menace would walk away with Silas's Perfect Bag That Was Clearly His Destiny.

A chill rolled down her spine. There was only one Silas Thorne, too. She'd fight the spirits, the Fae, and the entire forest to keep him safe.

Tabby watched her cousin's expression. "Don't worry, Briar. We'll get that cranky moose back."

Briar sniffed, holding back tears. "Yeah we will."

"Okay, so, what's the plan?"

"Well, it's a loose one," Briar answered, "because I'm still figuring it out. But the basic idea is to get to the gateway to Faerie, and somehow get in."

"You expect me to believe that you, Briar Whittaker, the ultimate planner, in this risky situation do not have a rock-solid plan?"

"I know. And believe me, I hate it. I am trying to plan out scenarios, but I don't know what we'll encounter. Plus I thought since you've spent way more time in Hollow Forest than I have, you might know what comes next and which direction it is."

"I don't know if that's true anymore, after your Lughnasadh tour de force," Tabby pointed out. "But I have gone deep in the forest and think I know which direction the portal is. I can probably get us there, but I have no idea how to get in."

"That's future us's problem. Present us needs to worry about getting there first."

Tabby gave her a dubious look that said enough. Flying blind into Hollow Forest right before the icy blast of Yule was set to hit could be filed under Insane Ideas and Questionable Life Choices. But, with Silas missing and it being clear that Briar was going in with or without help, Tabby dropped the doubt and went with sisterly trust instead. Tabitha opened a rift and started to step through. Once she was halfway in, she turned to Briar and held out her hand. "Get in, loser. We're going witching."

Briar had never hedge-ridden before. Although she was now an eclectic witch and had a few gray witch skills, she did not know how to enter the in-between and slip through to different places like Tabby did. Still, she had taken Tabby's hand and in she went, ready to take any shortcut opportunity to get to Silas quicker. But now that she was midway through their walk between the proverbial walls of the waking world and shadow realm, she started to worry about where they were going. She couldn't see any landmarks from what she would consider normal shit you see on a walk to identify the direction they were headed. Trees, rocks, even the ground. All of it was absent. Instead all she could see were streaky, black-and-white smudges rushing around her, like walking inside a watercolor. And the sound. It was like whipping wind, combined with a constant low-vibration tone. On top of that, there were walls, so it wasn't exactly "proverbial" because they walked in a narrow gap that felt like it wended on forever. She tried to ask Tabby a question, then realized she couldn't speak in there. Fun times.

As much as she wanted to exit the strange passage, she was well aware of how long she could stumble through the forest and possibly only find "something with teeth" as Silas always warned. Though at this point, Briar was so fired up and ready to brawl that she might be the one that ended up baring her canines at any dangers she came across.

Within what might have been a few minutes, she bumped into Tabby as they suddenly slid through a gap in the wall, which opened into the dark and frigid forest.

"Where are we?" Briar asked.

"The Northern Reaches. The entry might be somewhere around here."

Briar cringed. If Silas knew, oh he'd be *mad*. Or straight up worried. Because the Northern Reaches were synonymous with being lost in the woods, far from town. Populated by wild animals and even wilder spirits, it was a risk to be so far out. A frozen gust slammed into them from the north, as if the forest itself was saying "wrong way, sweetie."

"One guess as to which way it is," Briar muttered, teeth clacking as she braced against it.

For years she'd accepted the Yule storm as one of Willowmere's charming quirks. Now she knew better. The wind came straight from the heart of Hollow Forest, straight from the gate to Faerie.

Why it hit every year with the punctuality of a German train schedule? Still very much on her to-solve list.

The forest may have tried to push them south, to try and keep them from the gate. So naturally they headed straight into that icy blast.

Even with the jacket, hat, and scarf, the cold clawed its way through the layers eventually. The bitter and punishing wind howled and tore at them, as Briar and Tabby proceeded north. Though it wasn't the official storm, snowflakes pelted them and blew into their faces. Most normal people would take the hint, but it didn't deter them. Briar also used one of her recently acquired skills to warm their hands, she still couldn't light a candle with magic but at least she had learned a spell that enabled her to warm freezing flesh. It could be used to heat herself or someone nearby. With their current state, it was a welcome trick to have up her sleeve.

They pressed on like they were about to receive a warm welcome, even though it was obviously quite the opposite. The flashlight at least kept their path illuminated, a small respite against the unreal darkness. Fortunately, it seemed the cold even kept the restless spirits away, because there hadn't been any sign of otherworldly weirdness. Not that the cold bothered the spirits, but maybe they hadn't been prowling around, not expecting anyone to be so foolish as to be that deep in the woods.

Briar kept her face tucked into her scarf, only a small strip of her face was exposed, with snowflakes collecting in her eyelashes. What seemed at first like a flake glimmering in her lashes, reflecting the light of the flashlight as they walked, she then realized it was a light ahead of them on the path.

Tabby saw it, too. They both stopped and watched as a small, bluish light bobbed closer.

"Mirlah?" Briar called out.

"Excuse me? Was that a word?" Tabby asked.

"I think it's Mirlah, Silas's will-o-the-wisp."

"His what now? I knew there had been will-o-the-wisps seen in the forest, but never knew they might be someone's …pet."

"It's kind of a long story, but yes, apparently Mirlah was assigned to Silas, for lack of a better word, by his Fae mother. Silas is a bit secretive about it, about anything to do with his mother, so I never mentioned Mirlah to anyone else."

The blue light reached them and began circling Briar in tight, jittery loops—somewhere between excitement and alarm. Mirlah only communicated in fluttery vibes, and Briar could feel the little fairy's urgency thrumming in the air.

Mirlah drifted up to Tabby, inspecting the sliver of face visible between her scarf and hood.

"That's my cousin, Tabitha," Briar said. "She's helping me. Have you seen Silas? I think the Fae took him."

Mirlah bobbed up and down so decisively Briar almost felt winded just watching.

"Then take me to him! Can you help me open the portal?"

That sent her shooting backward, wings stuttering. Without Silas to translate, Briar was left to decipher spirals and swoops like some kind of panicked sky semaphore. Finally, Mirlah looped a curly *follow me* gesture, heading south.

Briar squared her shoulders and pointed north. "Nope. The gate's that way. If you're trying to lure me off on a side quest, I'm not going. I'm heading to the gate with or without your help."

Mirlah froze mid-air like a glitching firefly, then drifted back, slow and sulky. Giving the emotional equivalent of a guilty shrug. She would go, but she hated it. And she clearly didn't want Briar anywhere near that gate.

They pressed north, the wind no longer slamming into them like it had before. Now it only tugged at their coats, as if the storm had downgraded from actively hostile to mildly annoyed. Mirlah drifted farther behind with every step, her light shrinking to a sullen, shaky glow. Apparently even fairies had the good sense to dislike what waited ahead.

Then the forest opened, and Briar saw it.

A perfect circle of water hovered in the air, twelve feet tall and glowing like a suspended moon. Snow and sleet funneled out of it in a steady rush, streaking toward them before scattering into the clearing like the gate was exhaling directly onto their faces. The air around it buzzed, like it recognized her, and it was curious.

Awe hit Briar first, sharp and breath-stealing. Fear followed right behind it, crawling down her spine with cold fingers. She could feel the wrongness of the thing, the ancient weight of it.

But under all of that was something stronger. Her determination. Silas was beyond that threshold. That was all she needed to know.

It was crazy to think it had been earlier that same day that all she had to worry about were her Yule cake orders. Now she couldn't care less about that, her only concern now was Silas. Briar straightened her back and lifted her chin. "All right," she whispered, more to herself than anyone. "I'm coming."

And she stepped toward the gate.

Chapter 6

Moving into the water plane, she pushed against it, which resisted. Mirlah landed on her shoulder, which seemed to be the Faerie Express Pass, because Briar's foot popped through first. Tabby stepped forward to follow behind, but Mirlah jumped off of Briar, fluttering around Tabby and swishing an X through the air in front of her.

"I guess that means "no" in Mirlah speak," Tabby said, looking at Briar.

Without Mirlah touching her, Briar was forced to halt, leaving one foot on the other side of the portal. The gate wouldn't allow her to pass further. "Can you bring Tabby as well, Mirlah?"

The little ball of light zigzagged left to right, leaving no space to question whether she meant no.

Briar sucked in a breath. "Maybe she can't guide more than one person through the portal," she said to Tabby.

Mirlah zipped up and down.

"Well, fuck," Tabby said. "I'll be right here, Briar. You be careful, remember your strengths. And goals. Bring Silas back. If you forget everything else, remember that. Faerie can make you forget. Also don't eat the food they offer you, they can enchant you with it. Don't give them your name, and for Hecate's sake, don't make any deals with them. They are tricky bitches and will find a way to twist a deal so that they get what they want. Give me your hand."

Briar held her hand out to her cousin, who pulled a small pocket knife out. She carved a scratch into Briar's palm, then one into her own. Pressing the wounds together like some sort of ritual blood oath panini sandwich, Tabitha muttered a chant.

Mine to yours,
our blood as one.
Remember the goal,
see it done.
Trace the path
with steady focus.
And if you need it,
remember to hocus.

Briar winced at the cut, but nodded her agreement to Tabby. "Will you be okay?"

"I'll be fine, I can stay in the in-between while I wait, it'll protect me from the cold. I'll be able to hear you come back."

Hugging each other, they gave one last nod, before Mirlah rejoined Briar so she could pass between worlds.

Passing through the film was… an experience. One second she was suffocating in magical Saran Wrap, the next she was popping through it like a disgruntled cranberry in gelatin. Full-body heebie-jeebies achieved.

Then she looked around.

Yep. Figures. Faerie apparently subscribed to "magical winter Pinterest board" aesthetics. Snow everywhere, no cold whatsoever, and tiny glittering stars hanging in the air like they'd been placed there by an overcaffeinated decorator.

Briar looked at her hand, the cut had somehow already healed, but in its place was an iridescent scar which created intricate patterns on her skin. New world, new scar, who dis?

Mirlah wavered, the fairy equivalent of shaking in her boots.

"Well, come on, Mirlah. We might as well get going." Truth be told, if Briar was going based on her first impressions, the world was nothing short of breathtaking, and didn't feel dangerous in the slightest.

That probably should have been her first red flag.

As Briar walked through the strangely serene environment, she thought about Tabby's chant, about the spell she cast on her hand. It was a memory charm, one of Tabby's skills. As to what it all meant, she wasn't sure. "Remember the goal, see it done." Okay, that part was pretty clear. "Trace the path with steady focus." Don't get distracted? Or memorize the way? Maybe like Hansel and Gretel, drop some breadcrumbs to be able to retrace your steps. Some old-school fairytale hooey, but probably good advice.

Turning back to the portal to take a look at where she came from, she memorized the landmarks, the way the trees looked, the way the majestic far off purple mountains were shrouded in haze. And everywhere was *bright*. The realization hit her like a cold mist to the face on a sleepy morning. It had been darkest night when she stepped through, yet here was a brilliant, crisp day.

The air around her hummed, jittered. It was all fake, she could feel it. Everything she saw was an illusion. It had been so convincing at first, she thought it was like an idealized version of what Yule might *look* like if it were a place. There may as well have been giant candy canes stuck in the snow. She looked to her left, and wouldn't you know it, there they were. A whole field of red and white striped canes perfectly arched off in the distance, like it was a candy cane farm ready for a fun day of picking. "Nice try." She knew they weren't there before.

Briar turned again toward where she had come from, focusing on carving the memory of the portal area in her mind. It looked different from this side. It was so calm, the watery surface almost couldn't be seen, with no hint of the dark woods through the gate. And there was no wind or snow being funneled from this side into Hollow Forest. If the storm didn't originate here, where did it come from? This and other fun questions swirled in her mind, leaving her with one disturbing thought: since what she saw was apparently fake, she couldn't trust what she was seeing. Even if she memorized the area, it may not look like this the next time. If she needed the sights to help guide her, they could just as easily lead her astray.

Silas's bag suddenly felt heavy across her body. She had forgotten it was even there. Normally she wouldn't look inside, but with being in a weird realm and the even weirder thought that she couldn't believe her eyes, Briar decided to take a peek. A smile crept over her face as the first thing she saw was a croissant wrapped in a napkin, one of her Courage Croissants. She knew Silas usually smirked at the "courage" spell she added to it, bravery wasn't something that he usually lacked. But she also knew that it was one of his favorite things to snack on that she made daily. The other favorite being the Desire Danishes, which had gotten them into … situations, more times than once. *Spicy* situations.

"Well, the croissant is real." She took it out of the bag, then tore off a small bit. "The Hansel and Gretel method it is." Even if the surroundings changed, the croissant shouldn't. As long as it stayed put, that is. Dropping a piece on the ground, she muttered her hope that some little critter didn't come and steal it. It may do more good for her as a snack for later, but if there was even a slight chance it might help her find her way, it was worth committing the croissant to the cause. If it ended up as an offering to animals or some kind of Faerie spirit, then so be it.

Mirlah looped in the air, swishing to get Briar's attention.

"I take it it's time to hike?" Briar asked.

Mirlah bobbed.

"Fairy Swish says yes. Okay, let's go," Briar answered for her, striking out at a confident pace that would make any kids camp counselor proud.

Hiking through the pristine white snow was eerily easy. It shifted and flowed like sparkling miniscule crystals. As they passed between fragrant pine trees, Briar had a thought, the snow wasn't even cold. Swiping her hand into the blanket of undisturbed fresh powder, she lifted it to her mouth and touched her tongue to it.

"Sugar. It's fucking *sugar*. I don't even know why I'm surprised. I'm in a friggin' candy forest! Now I want to know who's making this. Show yourself!"

Mirlah zipped back to Briar, then clamped herself to Briar's mouth.

"I'm guessing speech is off-limits?" Briar muttered, words leaking past lips that Mirlah had held shut with all the subtlety of a magical clothespin.

The sugar-dusted paradise suddenly looked like it was designed by someone with a grudge. Lovely on the surface. Deadly underneath. And from the way Mirlah trembled, whoever built it was listening for more than compliments.

Silas, she needed to find Silas. The environment was a distraction, pure and simple. Or maybe a test, would Briar lose her way in this delicious-looking landscape? She nodded at Mirlah, then started walking again. There were questions she wanted to ask, but Mirlah's language barrier made getting straight answers difficult. And with listening ears somewhere unseen, she pressed her lips together, and pressed on.

It was some time later, perhaps hours, and they had been walking in circles. And that didn't mean the figurative version of walking in circles, because they had inadvertently walked right back to her Hansel and Gretl path. The surroundings looked different, but the breadcrumbs she had dropped remained. They had happened upon three croissant pieces previously tossed along the way, but were now in the middle of an unfamiliar, lush evergreen forest, the boughs flocked with snow. More like 'snow,' because the snow everywhere was still sugar, and the trees weren't real either. They were painstakingly carved chocolate, sprayed green, then dusted with more sugar to get the snowy effect. Even without touching them she could tell they were chocolate, she could *smell* them.

The thought of a smell being magic reminded her of Silas, and a pang of worry cleaved her heart. What if they kept her trudging through this illusion for an eternity? Having spirited Silas off to some corner of their realm where Briar didn't stand a chance to reach, then forced her to wander until she simply forgot him. Or if this was some sick joke, that she was somehow crisscrossing her own enchanted Yule cakes, her body shrunken down so small that she couldn't tell what she was walking on. They had altered her perception, who's to say they hadn't done something like that? "Ugh what if I get eaten by one of my own customers, on Yule no less. Not very celebratory." However, the fake snow and ice she saw in Faerie wasn't nearly as good as her own spell for sugar crystal snow. Silas had even said it was hard to tell it apart from real ice without tasting it.

The scent of the chocolate whipped up in a faint breeze, drawing her in closer. Tabby's warning replayed in her mind, telling her not to eat the food.

Briar waded through the white sugar, to the lowest branch of the chocolate tree nearby. She closed her eyes and steadied herself, preparing to break off a piece.

Mirlah's energy hummed in front of her, the little ball of light tried to push Briar back.

"I know, Mirlah, I think I know what it will do. But I also think it's the only way to change this cycle we are stuck in." The landscape was endless sweets, and the only way she could see them getting out of it was to accept being enchanted by eating what was apparently being offered.

Mirlah flickered, and sagged in the air like she resigned herself to agreeing with Briar.

Taking in one breath through her nose, she leaned forward and took a bite of the branch.

The chocolate melted on her tongue in a sumptuous moment,

the subtle crunch offset by a soft peppermint core. It was chocolat-ey perfection, and she savored it. Chewing once, twice, Briar swallowed, and the world tipped on its side.

Chapter 7

Fake snow streamed away from Briar, sugar funneled around her body, slipping through her fingers. The rush felt like quicksand, her hair tugging and fanning out like she lounged in water. Her head lolled, feeling weightless as she both fell and floated. The whole world fell down around her. Daydreams of glittering icicles, crystals and snowy magic flitted through her mind. It would have been blissfully peaceful if it wasn't so cold against her back.

Damn it was cold! It seeped in through her layers, negating the thickness of her jacket and chilling her to the bone.

Briar startled awake with a sharp inhale. She hadn't been truly asleep, but whatever trance she had been in ended in stunning, sobering clarity.

The smirks on the faces that peered down at her made Briar instantly regret taking a bite of that chocolate. Piercing, ice-blue eyes stared at her as she struggled to get her feet under her. Standing up to take everything in, she tried to look at everyone who stood on a dais overlooking the smooth floor she had been lying on. Realizing she was being watched by no less than ten people who had probably seen her swim on the pearly white floor? Not great. Noting that each of them were the most beautiful creatures she had ever seen? Even worse. These were somehow Fae gods and goddesses of the icy sort, and their disdain was evident as they watched her like an animal in a zoo. Briar looked past them to the walls made of carved ice, and the tall cathedral with arched windows, which opened to a chilly night. The diamond-like stars glittered on a velvety blanket of navy blue space. So it was still night, after all.

Murmurs swept through as Briar looked at everything. As she took in her surroundings, and the fact that she was most definitely placed intentionally on the lowest part of the floor while the already towering forms of the Fae spread around her, she recognized pretty damn quickly she was in way over her head. The very human phrase 'up a creek without a paddle' came to mind, though it would likely not make sense to any of the Fae that surrounded her. Because aside from being in a totally awkward position, she also had no friends present. Mirlah had apparently not been whisked out of the candy forest with her.

A commanding, feminine voice said, "Let me see her."

The crowd parted, and gave Briar a glimpse of a regal female wearing sparkling, pale blue robes which flowed over the throne she sat upon. Trimmed in white fur, with a silver spiked decoration reminiscent of a snowflake fanning up behind her, she stood then practically floated to the edge of the platform. So apparently Briar had been dropped straight into an ice queen's castle. Wonderful.

"Well, the mysterious intruder finally reveals herself," the female said, her voice carrying a chill that made Briar shiver.

Was everything fucking cold in this palace? Briar held herself steady and kept her mouth shut, mostly because she wasn't sure what to say, but also because she knew enough to be careful about what she gave away. She replayed Tabby's warnings in her head, trying to make sure she didn't allow the grandeur to dim the fact that she was now in the presence of some seriously untrustworthy creatures.

"Why have you breached the portal to Faerie without an invitation?" The queen's question echoed in the halls, the power of it somehow amplified. "Give me your name."

Hmmm yeah, the whole "plan" was going really well. The part where Briar thought in advance about how to handle questions like this was especially well-formulated. She hid her cringe at her obvious lack of preparation, which was so un-Briar-like to have no plan, then decided she had little choice but to say *something* before this queen decided to throw Briar into her frozen dungeon.

"Funny story! So I was walking in the forest and somehow ended up here. I don't—"

"—Skip to the part where you tell me who you are, and what you're doing here. I'm not interested in the lies of some human girl."

The other Fae around the queen folded their hands in front of them, their gazes hardening on Briar as if their stony looks alone could force the truth from her.

This was some next-level intimidation, the likes of which Briar had never experienced. In spite of the fact that her insides instantly became queasy and her blood went cold, because *of course* it did in this frigid place, she managed to feign confidence. "I'm here to find someone that was taken from my realm. I want them back, then I'll leave with no trouble." Briar faked a smile, but the feeling of relief was genuine because not only did she *not* cave to these beautiful bullies, she only gave enough information to not lie and still give them almost nothing. And also internally screaming a *hex no* to giving them her name.

A sly grin spread across the queen's face. "It's amusing to hear that you think you could leave here without trouble. You have *trespassed* on our land. You do realize you are now mine to do with as I will. Now, tell me your name."

Briar's breathing stopped. She had tried being cute. She tried being real but with a limited amount of information. Perhaps it was time to play the open heart card, to tell her why she had to come. "I'm here to find the man that I love. I've come to beg for his return. I'm desperate to get him back, and risked coming here in the hopes that I could be successful. Please, I'm begging you to let me go so that I may find him."

"Oh? Am I supposed to care that you love him? You know, I actually do appreciate when someone *loves*, it can be a wonderful motivator to get what I want. Because other than that, it's meaning-less."

Briar's mouth dropped. The way the queen enunciated "loves"

was like the very word repulsed her. She remembered Silas had told her once that the Fae don't truly love, it's something that is viewed as a means to an end to them. But to actually *hear* it, to be so unswayed by a person's pleas, it was a level of callousness that transcended the word itself. It was heartless. It was cold.

Cold.

Briar's face lit up with realization. Here was the ice queen of Faerie, standing a short distance from her. The one person in this realm who could do anything if she wanted to. Bad *or* good. And Briar, being a witch who was armed with the power to warm flesh, she might be able to use that to turn the queen to do good.

The power to melt a frozen heart.

Instead of responding to the queen's comments, or answering her demand to give her name, Briar turned her thoughts inward. She focused her intention on starting the spark within her, the warming force she could grow until it was strong enough to funnel to the queen. The queen kept talking, but Briar wasn't listening. She grew the spark until it was too large for her to contain, then sent her hands forward in a mighty push.

The orange glow overpowered the pale blue environment as it shot forward from her fingertips. Words died on the queen's lips when it struck her straight in the chest.

Briar heaved, smiling as her spell penetrated into the lustrous white skin of Her Royal Majesty, the Queen of Bitchy Comments.

The glow faded, and the bright, warm light retreated as Briar caught her breath.

Inspecting her nails, the queen asked, "Are you quite finished?" Sighing, she turned, then glided back to her throne, apparently unaffected in the slightest bit. "I have better things to do than to entertain weak magic from a silly girl. Though, good to know you have magic. You may be useful to me."

Briar practically crumpled, the spark did *nothing*, and it had taken nearly all of her strength to create.

Settling back into place on her throne, the queen adjusted her robes, barely interested in Briar's current state of shock and disappointment. "Don't be so dramatic, you couldn't have expected that to work on me, could you?"

"It was supposed to melt your frozen heart," Briar said, looking at her hands. Her spell had failed miserably.

The queen laughed. "You can't melt what isn't there. Now that you've proven to yourself the futility of fighting against me, I'll once again *demand* you give me your name."

Hope faded. Briar had nothing, no ideas for another spell, no tricks to get herself out of there. She did have one bargaining chip, though. "I want to make you a deal."

The queen perked up. "A bargain? I do enjoy a good bargain."

Briar gulped. This was dangerous territory. A deal with the Fae was specifically what Tabby told her not to do. And she was going to double up on checking off items from the 'Things Not To Do In Faerie' list. "I'll give you my name if you give me the chance to find my love."

The queen flicked her hand, batting away the offer. "Not

nearly enough. Your name isn't worth *that* much." She waited, staring at Briar, not moving, and giving no indication of what she was thinking.

"We have planning to do," a male to the queen's left said, "it's time to move this along."

The queen quirked her lip in a disapproving twist, motioning to him that she would do so momentarily. Shifting her head slightly back to Briar, she said, "I have a counteroffer for you. Give me your name, *willingly*, then go on a quest for me."

What in the tabletop role playing game fresh hell was this? A quest for the ice queen? "What do you want me to do?"

"Seek someone out. An individual formerly of my court, who refuses to submit to my will and do my bidding. Find him, and convince him to return to my castle, return *to me*. Do these two things, and you may seek out your love."

"*And* I can bring my boyfriend back to the human world when I find him," Briar amended. "And! If you know where he is, you must show him to me."

The queen rolled her eyes. "Agreed. Now, if you fail to find whom I want returned…." Her slow grin revealed gleaming white canines. "If you fail, you agree to stay here for as long as I wish, and do my bidding in his stead."

And there it was. The dark part of the deal Briar somehow knew would get wrapped in there. She half expected it to be an unsaid part that she would discover later. It was *almost* commendable how un-Evil Queen she was being by being above board. Almost.

"Agreed."

A gong rang, startling Briar nearly off of her feet. Who even had a gong? But as that note struck again, and then struck a third time, she felt a burning sensation on her hand. She looked, and discovered a new tattoo inked in deep blue on the back of her hand. An intricate snowflake emblazoned with a four-pointed star embedded within the design, the tall center point reached up her middle finger, the opposite one ended below her wrist. Fine bands circled her fingers, like delicate ink rings.

Shackles. Nothing like an involuntary tattoo to seal the deal.

"Now, your name."

"Briar Marie Whittaker."

The moment her name was off of her lips, it was like a brisk wind snatched it away, no longer hers. The queen grabbed at the unseen wind, picking the invisible words out of the air and wrapping her fingers around them, then tucked them into a hidden pocket inside of her robes.

"Now go," the queen commanded.

Briar opened her mouth to ask questions, but a massive door down the hall opened, letting in a blustering swirl of snow and wind. As she turned back to the dais, she realized she had been instantly transported to the outside, then the doors swung shut with a clang and locked her out alone.

"Well that was rude."

Chapter 8

Standing outside the doors to the imposing ice castle, Briar waited for a few minutes, trying to get her bearings in the cold night. She didn't know which way to start out. With no idea where Silas even was, she had made a foolhardy deal with a cold queen, and was now on the losing end of a deal that could change the course of her very life. Instead of thinking about the growing number of difficulties she now faced, she decided she had to fix the current problem of being unprepared in an unpredictable winter environment … in a magical land that could trick her, no less. Pulling herself up by her shoulders and trying desperately to not fall into despair, she forced herself to look around and decide her next course of action.

"Definitely feeling *super great* about all of this," she said to no one.

Turning on the spot, she noted that she was surrounded by barren, snowy hills, the palace seemingly in the middle of nowhere. With no clue what to do to make good on this bargain, she started walking. North seemed as good as any direction to head in. Plus the area to the south looked to be white out conditions. It's always nice when a possible direction looks nothing short of hazardous to help you decide which way *not* to go. Yay positive thinking.

After a few hours of hiking, a spot in the distance caught her eye. Glowing bright and blue, a tiny orb zipped through the snow flurries, straight to Briar. Mirlah circled fast in haphazard shapes around Briar as she arrived, clearly sending a message of relief and joy. And maybe a touch of fairy hysteria. Briar smiled at the tenacious little sprite, grateful that she had found her again.

"I know, Mirlah, you tried to warn me. I may have really done it now. And … don't be pissed. I made a deal with the ice queen."

Mirlah's light guttered and she fell away in an exaggerated impression of fainting.

"Wow, someone can act," Briar muttered. She would have laughed, if the situation wasn't so dire. "So here's the thing, while I agree it was probably a hasty decision to eat the chocolate tree, a bad idea to make a deal, and an even worse mistake to give her my name … this is what we have to deal with now. I know, I know, both Silas and Tabby would have serious words for me right now, and Silas would probably be beyond worried that I am now here *and* in the midst of a bargain with this queen. He never told me about her, but I could guess what he might say. All of that aside, I have to follow through on what I agreed, or I'm cooked. If I fail I'll be stuck here as her ... I don't know what, servant?"

Mirlah swayed left to right, Briar figured it was equal to wringing her hands.

"Yeah, not great. But maybe you can help me. I have to find some ... *person*, a Fae? I don't even know. Ugh she has set me up to fail! I was going to ask her for more details when she kicked me out of the castle. All she said was someone that used to be part of her court but now refuses to do her bidding or go to the castle. She gave me zero information aside from that. Wait ... she said "find *him*" so we at least know that."

Mirlah lifted, her light blinking rapidly.

"Do you have an idea of who it might be?" Briar couldn't help the spark of hope that ignited within her. Mirlah swished through the air, indicating a path that headed west.

Briar followed Mirlah's light for hours, a welcome beacon in the dark night. Fortunately she still had Silas's bag, and when they started the hike she still had water and a bit of croissant left. Now she regretted dropping pieces previously because the croissant was gone, and she only had one sip of water left. At least she could keep herself warm enough, though it expended more energy to consistently drum up enough of a spark to make any sort of noticeable barrier against the biting cold.

Briar wondered if this was the storm that would stir into a frenzy, then blast its way through the portal. Walking for so long left her too much time to let her thoughts wander, because her mind jumped from one worry to another: Silas and wherever he was, Tabby sitting in the in-between waiting for Briar to come back, herself and whether or not she'd get stuck in Faerie. She needed a change in scenery, otherwise she'd drive herself mad with the what-ifs.

Trees appeared ahead of her, and Mirlah perked up, speeding along her midair path through them.

"Wait up, Mirlah!" Briar pumped her arms, trying to get her feet to run through the snow. It was difficult running with boots made for walking. And not just walking, but walking on an easy-going sidewalk. Not for hiking, in the snow, in a treacherous magical world with constantly falling snow. What if the ice queen had a cloud over Briar snowing on just her? That would track.

Mirlah slowed, making sure Briar could see her, before moving further into the trees. Briar squinted, and eventually saw a warm light deep within. Her stomach bottomed out at the sight. An actual *light*, like a lantern, giving off a warm glow. Warmth in this place? Even the light associated with the queen was cold. This had to be something different.

Suddenly she found she could run in her boots, it only took the right motivation. She pushed her legs faster, moving the snow in great strides. Her breath heaved as she arrived, finding the light was hung on a wooden wall next to a heavy wood door with huge iron strap hinges. Nothing about it was intricate, no ornate filigree like the Fae seemed to be obsessed with doing. Briar pounded on that strong, utilitarian door.

Boots thudded across the floor inside. "Who is it?" a gruff, gravelly voice asked.

Mirlah hung back and quaked.

Briar side-eyed her, now worried about *whose* door she was so loudly knocking on. She had barely given that a thought when she saw it. But, she was on one side, in the cold, hungry, and now needing water. Plus there was the whole pesky matter of settling a bargain with an impossibly demanding queen. Circumstances being what they were, she was going to have to win over whoever this was.

"I'll ask again! Who is it?" his voice boomed.

"My name is …." *Oh hex!* She tried to say it, tried again, but it wouldn't come out.

"I won't open the door unless I know who you are. Now go away and leave me in peace."

"Please! Please open the door. I'm trying to say my name, but it isn't mine anymore."

He paused, and all sound stopped. Briar waited, clenching her fists readying to pound the door again. Even if she couldn't give her name, she had to come up with a way to convince him to let her in.

"Now don't tell me you gave it to *her*," he said and laughed darkly.

She heard another footstep as he started to walk away. Briar wound up her fist to hit the door. She swung right as the door opened, her balled fist landing square on his sternum with a thud.

"Oh ... I am so sorry," she fumbled. "I thought you were walking away." She awkwardly smoothed the shirt of the absolute beast of a man, tall and broad shouldered.

"... You're a girl," the man said.

"Woman," Briar corrected. "But yes."

"I mean you're human. You're not one of them. What on earth are you doing here?"

Briar squinted her eyes, trying to make out his features, but the light from inside backlit him and made him difficult to see. "Are you not one of them?"

His thick, gloved hand wrapped around hers, as he pulled her inside, then let go of her hand. He shut the door, snowflakes swirling for a moment at the jamb, before the wind was snuffed out and the heat from the wood cabin warmed her face. He turned, letting the light catch his features.

Chapter 9

Briar stared at the man who had just pulled her into his cabin. His nut brown hair, his thick, arched eyebrows, and honey-gold eyes were unmistakeable. And his lumberjack mode was set to one hundred, with his scruffy beard and plaid shirt.

"You're Sawyer Thorne," she breathed. "You haven't been seen in over thirty years." In actuality she'd never seen him herself, Briar hadn't even been born by the time he disappeared, she only knew what he looked like.

"Sounds about right," he said. "I take it that means you're from Willowmere."

She nodded, half-afraid to say the most important part about who he was. She sucked in a breath, mustering the courage. "And you're Silas's dad."

His face hardened. "What do you know of my boy?"

"A lot," she admitted.

He motioned to a small couch by the fire, covered in dark green plaid. Of course more plaid. The apple doesn't fall far from the tree, a tree which father and son would have likely cut down together. They both had the same Woodland Lumber Expert trademark. She followed him to the couch, then sat at the same time he did.

"I'm his girlfriend."

His eyes widened, a pleased expression crossed his face for a moment, which was then replaced by something else. Distrust? Doubt? Something didn't add up for him.

"You're telling me Silas allowed you to give your name to his mother?" he asked, his tone nearly accusatory.

She shot up to standing. "His what now? Are you telling me his *mother* is the ice queen of Faerie?"

He motioned for her to sit again. "Well right now she's the ice queen, but come spring she'll be the spring queen and have stuff growing everywhere, then summer and so on. She changes with the seasons. She's at her strongest in the winter, though, most of her family line comes from the Winter Court. It also makes her exhausting to be with."

Briar rubbed her eyes. "Okay, the every season queen and kinda mostly winter then. But you're telling me that was his mother?"

He nodded. "So I guess that means you don't know quite as much about him as you thought."

Ouch. Shots fired. That comment speared Briar's heart. "Well now I know where Silas gets his blunt curmudgeon side from."

Sawyer smirked. "Ha, yeah you got me there, Missy. But really I'm giving you a hard time, because a lot of it he's not able to say, even if he wanted to."

"Wait, if that's his mother ... oh hex. Wow, she tricked me. She never let on that Silas was there in the castle, or that she knew anything about him." Briar replayed the encounter, the way she professed her love. It was of course obvious who Briar was looking for, but Briar didn't think to ask the right questions, and the queen had taken advantage of it.

"Yeah, well, she's good at tricking people," Sawyer said. "She's very cunning. Another thing about her that's exhausting. She's always calculating something. Now let me see if I have this straight, Silas doesn't know you're here? Or he does, but you don't know where he is?"

"I don't know if he does know that I'm here, I came looking for him when he went missing. He was acting really weird the last few days, then suddenly disappeared. I went to his house and found a Fae arrow shot into his door with a note I couldn't read on it. As far as I can tell, they took him against his will."

"Hmm, yeah, sounds like his summons finally came in," he commented as he rubbed his beard, still wearing his thin gloves. "Once she has her mind made up, she won't listen to anyone's wishes. She must've finally set her deadline. I wonder why she chose to do it now."

"What does that mean, what summons?"

He paused, then gave her a knowing look. "I'll let you think about that for a moment, think about who she is, as in her title, and that he's her son, and what that would make him."

"... Please tell me it's not an arranged marriage."

"Bingo, unfortunately. But think of it this way. The Fae are all about contracts, all about the rules governing their little deals. It seems to me that contracts are possibly the most important thing to them. It's a big reason why Silas left in the first place. He had no intention of being forced into that, and I agreed with him. Hence me being here."

Briar wanted to break down and cry. No wonder the queen had taken advantage of Briar's ignorance, she had something that she intended to force Silas to do, and a witch girlfriend would only get in the way. "I can't believe he didn't tell me *any* of this. Nothing about who his mother really was, nothing about an arranged marriage."

"Hey, I know this sucks," he said, patting Briar's hand, then held it there, keeping it in place for warmth and comfort. "Nobody wants to hear that their boyfriend has been obligated to marry someone else. This is the type of shit the Fae do, and they don't care about who it hurts. It's the contract above all else. And like I said, a lot of it he couldn't say. He's been restricted with something akin to magical restraints. Just like you can't say your name now. The queen holds the power."

Sawyer moved his hand away, and Briar felt a cold pang of loss at the motion. For the first time in decades, she had a fatherly figure's presence near her. She didn't even know this guy, and yet she already felt a connection to him. Her own dad had been removed from her life when she was a child, and rightly so because of the wrongs he had done. Yet it was a void she always carried. In spite of the situation being absolutely heart wrenching, she was glad to have found Silas's dad. She looked at where he had placed his hand, the tattoo now glaring at her.

His eyes drifted to where she stared. Sawyer's mouth dropped open when he saw the snowflake-and-star design. "Oh tell me you didn't. You made a *deal* with her?!" He stood and raked his fingers through his hair, then started pacing.

Briar gulped. "Yep. I did."

"Oh my God. Do you have any idea ...."

"I know, it was not what I wanted to do. But I was in a real bind. A bind by her design, obviously. She had claimed I trespassed on her land, and said I was already hers to do with as she pleased. I had been stuck in some fake candy forest, walking for hours. I had to break the cycle by accepting something to eat. I'm sure she had me from that moment."

"This is a real shitstorm, missy. So ... what are the terms?"

Briar cringed. "You're really not going to like it." She laid out everything, including the details that involved him. He rubbed his temples so hard she thought any headache he had massaged away was likely worse from using too much pressure.

"Well, this is definitely not how I expected this evening to go. Okay, first thing's first I suppose. Let's figure out your name. I can't very well keep calling my son's love Missy."

"How can I give you my name? Also, I'm not sure it's fair to call me your son's love either."

"Aren't you?"

"Well, I think so. But he's never actually told me that he loves me, and vice versa. He certainly *shows* me he does. But we've only been dating a few months. I had planned on telling him during our Yule celebration ... I can't believe I'm telling his dad all of this."

Sawyer chuckled. "Need I remind you that you professed your love for him to his mother as well?"

Briar froze. "Oh *hex*, I did."

"You know I must admit I'm surprised a girl like you would go through so much effort and take so much risk for someone who hasn't laid out how he feels about you. You're really going out on a limb without that reassurance."

"Nice lumberjack pun."

He laughed. "Well I am serious."

Briar looked thoughtful. "It's not surprising to me, I didn't even second guess that I would risk everything to come and help him. Love is about actions, not words. He's shown me with his actions every day what I mean to him, with big things and little gestures. Silas has never failed to do so once. So this is me showing with my actions what he means to me. And someday, I'll use the words as well to tell him. I only hope I get the chance to do it."

Sawyer got a wistful look in his eye. "My son is very lucky. Not everyone has that selfless love from a partner. I'm glad he has you." He looked away and sighed, detaching from the moment. It seemed to Briar like he slipped far away from his cabin, looking off in the direction she had come from. His expression changed, becoming more serious. "So, time to figure out your name, Missy."

The sudden return to the present snapped Briar out of her thoughts. "But how? It's like it wouldn't come out of my throat when I tried to tell it to you."

"I've learned a few workarounds. Now, does your name start with an A?"

Briar's eyes flew open, shaking her head "no". When he asked her if it started with a B, she found she couldn't answer, not even a head shake.

"There we go, B," he grinned. "Next letter."

"Wait," she said, thinking through everything the queen said. "You said it's all about the contract with the Fae, right?"

Sawyer nodded.

"My agreement was that I gave her my name *willingly*. Granted I didn't realize what that meant, that it was literally hers now. But what if she could use the technicality of you figuring out my name by how I respond to guessing each letter? What if she could use that to say I invalidated our contract and she didn't have to hold up her end of it?"

"Hmm, that is a good point. Okay, B it is, it'll be my nickname for you until I earn the right to the full version." He gave her a crooked grin. "And don't worry. I may be a log-headed lumberjack with more enthusiasm than finesse, but I'm not about to let that queen waltz into Silas's life and freeze things over. We're getting that deal handled so you two can get home." He stood, moving toward the door. "Let's get going. No time like the present."

"Shouldn't we plan what our next move will be?" Briar asked, but got up as well.

He reached the door, opened it and looked at the snowy trees ahead, the warm light of his house rim lighting him against the cold, dark blue night. Looking back at Briar, he shook his head slowly. "There's no way to foresee what might happen. If I'm going to go back there, I at least want it to be an adventure getting there. And if I've learned one thing from the forest, it's that adventure begins when plans end."

Who knew lumberjacks could be such cinematic drama queens.

Chapter 10

Snow blew in flurries around their boots as they hiked. Mirlah hung close to Briar, though she seemed unaffected by the cold. There had been a moment when Sawyer and the little fairy first saw each other, a tentative, uncertain greeting. But after an awkward pause and an even more awkward hello, they seemed to be content to pass each other off as moderately acceptable company. Briar could guess that Sawyer didn't like that Silas had one of the queen's will-o-the-wisps assigned to follow him, and was now attached at Briar's shoulder.

The thought gave her pause. Why was Mirlah with her, and why had she only now questioned that? Was Mirlah with her because Silas was worried about Briar? That would mean Silas would have *known* Briar would come after him. If he thought to ask Mirlah to keep an eye on Briar and keep her safe. This and other uncomfortable questions swirled in her head as they walked. Also churning was the unsettling possibilities of what could happen once they reached the castle. Would this resolve her bargain? And what would happen to Sawyer? Granted he had more than willingly accompanied her with the knowledge that the queen wanted him back as part of her court, Briar had been clear about what the deal was. He accepted it as much as Briar had. That part had been surprisingly easy, almost too easy, she had expected to find someone who would need a hex of a lot more convincing. And hexxing is precisely what she had been prepared to do if needed.

"So Miss B, what do you do in Willowmere?"

She took a sip of water, buying herself time before she had to answer. Fortunately she had remembered before they left his cabin her canteen was basically out, and made Sawyer take a few minutes to fill up before they began their journey. An adventure's no good if you dehydrate on the trail. "I own a local bakery in the village called Bun Intended, Silas helps me every morning with it." She sucked in a breath, realizing this was the point where good ol' dad gets to know his son's mystery woman, and since he knew Willowmere, that also might mean he might know certain things.

"And I take it you're a witch."

Well that didn't take long. "Yes, I am." She decided against adding any extra information or comments to the statement. No indication of worry, or feelings of concern about the question. Because in truth she had feared he would ask exactly this, and given that he was Silas's dad, and Silas had his own initial disbelieving thoughts about the witches of Willowmere, she worried he shared the sentiment.

"You gave it away, that's all. You said "hex" more than once.

Only the witches ever used that word in the way you did."

"… I did do that, didn't I? Can't keep a witch from witching, I guess."

"I always liked them, the witches, that is. The ones I knew were always helpful, and skilled."

Briar blew out a breath, she hadn't realized how tense she had been only moments before, holding her breath and waiting for the other shoe to drop. Waiting for that slanted comment about her beliefs and her sisters. "You know for being a log-headed lumber-jack, you're okay."

He laughed. "Well thanks for the approval, Miss B."

"So, what do you do, way out here all alone? How do you fill your days?" she asked.

"I'm actually pretty busy, I have a job."

"You do?!" She turned to look at him, surprised that there would be work of some kind out in the sticks of Faerie.

"Yeah, I'm the local branch manager." He lifted his hands, motioning at all the trees surrounding them.

"Lumberjack dad jokes, now *that's* a new one for me," Briar said, chuckling.

"Dad jokes. I almost forgot about those. Being separated from the human world … you forget things."

Briar looked at him sidelong. His joking manner had shifted to a somber tone. "What are your best memories of it?"

Sawyer smiled, talking about things he remembered he loved. He told her how had played drums in a Grunge garage band in the neighboring town of Granite Pass, a forty minute drive he used to make with his beat up old Ford. His only friends had been there, and probably didn't have any clue how to find him if they tried to look for him in Willowmere. He mentioned he had been a loner in their town, and when the queen crossed the portal and beckoned him to join her, he couldn't help but fall for her. Though at the time he hadn't known her rank, she had simply seemed like a young, beautiful Fae female who only wanted companionship. *His* companionship. Given that it had been Beltane, the fire festival centered on fertility and celebrates the rite of spring, Briar could figure out the rest. Sexual energy practically sizzled every Beltane Eve in Hollow Forest, he didn't have to tell her that part to know that fact. She could see how it was a perfect convergence for a human like him to end up choosing that path.

"Do you miss it? Willowmere, that is," Briar asked.

"Sometimes. But a lot of what I loved there is here. The forest, the ability to live near nature. It's lonely, that's for sure. But I don't have the human world pressures. Bills, taxes, all of that, it's nonexistent in Faerie. Also nonexistent is modern conveniences, like grocery stores. Food can be difficult, or it would be, but I manage. I get a supply every few months."

"Supply? From where? Like a co-op or food sharing system? Do they have that?"

"No, not like that. It just shows up. Wooden boxes of grain, meat, jerky, jars of preserved fruits and vegetables, various random supplies. All kinds of things. It appears near my house every season."

She thought for a second. "It's from her, isn't it? She sends it."

He nodded. "I think so, but it's never announced, and it's sent without a note. It's just there. In addition to that, I garden. I grow my own vegetables in a nearby field."

Briar lit up. "I love gardening. I'm a green witch, and gardening is one of my great loves."

"A green witch, huh? So you can help the plants take root, grow, all of that."

She nodded. "Well, really I'm an eclectic witch, because I'm also equally a kitchen witch, hence my bakery, but I grow my own herbs and spices I use to bake with. Time in the garden is one of the most peaceful parts of my day. Baking can be a little like creating with chaos, there's usually a lot going on and customers to manage. Gardening is where I spend my quiet moments."

They lost themselves in conversation as their boots crunched the snow. She told him the story of their harvest holiday, Lughnasadh, and her hair-brained idea to enter the shadow realm in Hollow Forest for answers about her mother. She told Sawyer about what Silas did, that before she went into Hollow Forest they had been adversarial. But when he came to help her and he helped her get home, their relationship had shifted and blossomed.

A chill wind rushed through, making both Briar and Sawyer shiver. "Here," she said, stopping to face him. "I have a little trick I can do." She focused inward, growing a spark to warm them. Within moments, she created a soothing warmth that enveloped them both. "It should last for a little while to ward off the cold."

"That's some trick," he said, shaking off the last of the chill.

Briar couldn't hide her triumphant smile, the fatherly praise filling a vacant spot in her soul. "It's a new spell for me. All of my magic is based on warmth. Certainly comes in handy since we're in a frozen land!"

Mirlah floated closer, her light pulsing. The interruption earned a glare from Sawyer. The little sprite swished through the air away from them, making her "this way" motion.

"You sure you trust that sparkle pest?" Sawyer asked once Mirlah was out of earshot.

"Pest? It's not like she's some termite that's going to eat your precious wood," Briar joked. "I think I trust her. She's helped me a bunch of times, and Silas likes her."

Sawyer raised his eyebrows.

"Okay, *mostly* likes her. He doesn't dislike her, but he doesn't like that she's been forced by his mother to be with him. He wants her to have autonomy."

"I don't really dislike her either, but listen to your own words. "Forced by his mother." That creature is under the queen's command, so what do you think she's doing here with you? I'll give you a one word answer. *Assigned.*"

Briar frowned. She had worried why Mirlah was there, but ultimately, Mirlah had helped her countless times. If she was assigned by the queen, then why did Mirlah help rather than hinder? "Sure, maybe she's assigned to watch me," Briar said, "but I'd argue that if that's the case, Mirlah has strayed to the limits of what she's allowed to do in order to help me." Briar decided that it did little good to question Mirlah's motivations, and had to go on actions alone. Mirlah had helped up until then. That was going to have to be enough for now. "Come on, let's get going."

Several hours later, they reached the forest's edge, where the slanted rim of the valley floor met the treeline. Briar felt it like a pressure behind her ribs, the threshold of everything that was to come. Once they stepped out from beneath the branches, it would be open plains straight to the castle. If the night weren't so ink-black, she suspected she'd already see its towers glittering like frozen teeth on the horizon.

"Well," Briar said, exhaling slowly, "our adventure wasn't exactly daring …but I liked getting to know you."

Sawyer let out a warm, rumbling chuckle. "I didn't expect daring. She wanted me back in one piece. Knowing her, she probably cleared half the dangers from our path just to make sure nothing slowed us down."

Briar frowned. "But earlier you said you wanted one more adventure before returning to her court."

"I did." He shifted, turning toward her fully. "The adventure wasn't in dodging danger. It was talking to you. Hearing about Silas. Learning who he's become." His voice softened. "And learning who *you* are to him."

Her breath hitched.

He glanced away, jaw tight but not bitter. "I haven't seen my boy in eight years. If he returned, the contract would trap him. And I can't cross back into Willowmere. So this—" he gestured between them, "—was my way of being part of his life again, even if only for a few hours."

A pang spread warmth through Briar's chest. "Mr. Thorne ..."

He shrugged, humble as ever. "I may be a log-headed lumber-jack, but I know when something matters. And what you and Silas have? That matters more than any old Fae contract. I know plenty about them, I had one myself."

For a long moment, the vast, cold quiet surrounded them, waiting to be broken.

Briar looked toward the plains, imagining her bakery windows lit for Yule, the smell of cinnamon rolls, Tabby's occasional pranks, the warm life she and Silas had been building without even realizing it. And how easily it could all be stolen.

She set her shoulders. "Then I guess it's my turn to bring him home. Back to Willowmere. Back to Yule. Back to everything that's ours."

Sawyer nodded, steady and certain. "Adventure starts where plans end. Remember that."

Briar gripped Silas's satchel and stepped toward the darkness stretching before them.

"Then let's end *her* plan."

Chapter 11

Massive, frozen doors that were all too familiar loomed directly in front of Briar and Sawyer. It had happened too fast, they crossed the plains, then walked up to the entrance that stood ten men tall. The doors swung open for them, and waited.

Their only greeting was a gust of snow and wind. Icy flooring, frost covered walls. No Fae stood near the entrance, no queen to bade them in.

"She's nothing if not dramatic," Sawyer muttered.

"Well, here we go." Briar grabbed his gloved hand and gave it a squeeze, searching for reassurance. Having zero scraps of a plan made her uneasy, but Sawyer had a point before they left his cabin. He had said there would be no way to foresee what would happen. She nodded to herself, giving *herself* that reassurance. They would have to rely on their wits and their strengths. It was as simple as that. The queen had the upper hand, all they could do was play into it with the best of their abilities.

The air flurried around them, blinding them with snowflakes.

As the area cleared, she saw they had been whisked into the throne room again, shortcutting whatever passages lay between the entrance and here. Which also meant, they didn't know the way back out.

Briar gulped as she looked up to the queen, sitting as still as stone on her throne and surrounded by tall, slender Fae as before. Formal and cold like they were observing suspects, they watched Briar and Sawyer with piercing, unflinching gazes. Flanking the queen , they stood rigid with five on each side of her like a murder of crows plotting revenge.

Waiting to speak, Briar held her tongue as the queen and Sawyer's gazes locked.

"So, you've returned, Briar Whittaker, and brought the missing member of my court."

The sound of her name on the queen's lips stole Briar's breath. The queen's eyes shifted to Briar's, the power of it boring into her. It took effort to lift herself before speaking. "Yes, Your Highness. He has come willingly with me at your request, which means I have satisfied the terms of our bargain."

One of the stately Fae hissed. "Be done with this already, Maeve. You have your court member back. Get rid of the girl so we may get on with our plans. She is delaying us before Yule descends."

The queen flashed a glance to the one who spoke, and Briar didn't fail to notice that he had used a name for her. She hadn't heard *anyone* speak it, not when she had been in the castle previously, Sawyer hadn't said it either, and Silas had always avoided the subject.

The look on the queen's face for half a moment carried something, a micro-expression that Briar almost missed. *Worry.* Maeve waved a hand, the subtle tell already washed away. "You have met my terms, Briar Marie Whittaker."

"Our bargain was that you would tell me where my boyfriend is, and let us go."

A cold, humorless smile crossed her face. "So it was. Send for Silas."

"Why Silas? He is not needed yet," the overbearing Fae male asked. "The marriage ceremony is not until tonight."

"Why should I not call my son for dealings of the court, Lord Casimir?"

He bared his teeth, but said nothing further as a small ball of light materialized from somewhere near the throne, then disappeared down the hall. Another one of the queen's will-o-the-wisps rushed off to do the queen's bidding.

Briar's heart was in her throat, and she could feel Sawyer struggling to keep his breathing even, too. Hearing that the marriage ceremony was that evening sent a wave of panic through her. But something was off, Briar sensed it hanging in the air, permeating the space. Lies, misdirection, she could *feel* it. Briar couldn't wait to finally lay eyes on Silas, but dreaded what would happen in the moments after. Somehow, the queen had a trick up her sleeve and Briar knew it. Did Maeve intend to weasel out of the deal and force her to watch Silas marry another? Or was it some trick to force

Briar into servitude?

It only took moments before she heard him coming, felt him nearing her, and she could have cried out on the spot. Silas appeared on the dais next to his mother, then looked down at Briar. Their connection was electric as they stared at each other. To finally find him, to see him and know he was safe, it eased her heart at least a little, in spite of the fact that there were a whole bunch of jerks in the room that wanted him to be with someone else. Memories of their life together came flooding back, how they spent their days, and their nights. The thought that she might not have any more of those was a gut punch she could have done without. There was no realm where she'd let someone take that from them, even if she had to do something drastic to protect it.

His gaze finally shifted to her left, and his expression pulled back in surprise as he saw his father. Silas looked like his knees were about to buckle. Looking back at Briar, his jaw feathered, and his nostrils flared like he held himself back from unleashing on anyone near him. But it wasn't anger in his eyes, it was terror, and pain. "What's the meaning of this, mother?" he shouted.

Lord Casimir shot a suspicious glance between Maeve and Briar.

The queen stood. "Briar Marie Whittaker has made a deal for you, son. She has done as I asked, and returned your father to court."

"A deal for *him?*" Lord Casimir bellowed. "There was no mention of this when the deal was struck. She never said it was

Silas, we would never have let you make that bargain. You could not agree to this deal, Maeve! You know very well Silas was already under a binding contract with *my court*." The other Fae near him bristled, conferring with each other in hushed whispers. Lord Casimir turned to talk to them, growing more agitated as they discussed.

Maeve looked back to Briar, and Briar saw that millisecond micro-expression again. *Worry. Pleading.*

Briar summoned her courage. "Queen M—" Briar opened her mouth wider, trying to say her name, but she couldn't. It wouldn't come out, the queen's true name was stuck in her throat. Briar's sight line snapped to Lord Casimir. She realized she couldn't say her name because *he* had the power over it. Clarity resolved further, he had said Silas was under contract with his court, meaning a different one from Queen Maeve's. "Your Highness," Briar continued as quickly as she could, "I have completed the terms of our bargain. I will take Silas now."

"You will *not*," Lord Casimir ordered. "He is to stay here and fulfill his duty."

"I will not stay!" Silas shouted back. "I already abdicated, what good does forcing me to marry your heir do you?"

Briar clenched her fists, racking her mind for what to do. She squeezed her hand so hard, the scar on her palm throbbed, the one from the memory charm Tabby had done. *Tabby*, she had almost forgotten her, and forgotten the spell she wove for Briar before she entered the portal. The last line of it flashed in her memory.

And if you need it,
remember to hocus.

To hocus, *to trick*. "If I can't have him, no one will," Briar declared. She thrust her hand toward Silas, mustering all her strength to cast a spell over Silas to encase him in ice.

It grew around his feet first, blossoming out in rapidly expanding, rigid crystals. It spread up his legs in less than a second, quickly overtaking his body before he even had a chance to move.

"No!" The queen cried out.

Lord Casimir stepped in, raising his palm to try and negate Briar's power. "What is this magic?" He struggled to have any effect on it as Briar continued to funnel her strength into the spell.

The crystals formed around Silas's shoulders, then crept up his neck. The formations fanned upward and reached his chin, spread onto his perfectly formed lips that were parted ever so slightly, then swept onto his tongue which touched the crystals for a moment. Their gazes locked on each other, Silas's eyes softening as he looked at her. "Goodbye, my silly witch."

Briar almost lost her resolve at those words. "Goodbye, my wild moose. I'm sorry."

"Miss B! What are you doing?" Sawyer shouted.

Briar looked over at Sawyer, holding her hands steady to maintain the spell, and shook her head "no." She knew she had crossed a line, locking Silas in place and enshrouding him to prevent him from marrying another definitely looked like jealous girlfriend behavior. "I'm doing what must be done," she ground out through clenched teeth.

The ice rushed over the rest of Silas's head, crackling as it encased him completely.

Lord Casimir hollered, cursing at Briar and his incapable party of Fae attendants.

"My Lord, if he dies before you terminate the contract, we can't renegotiate!" another Fae standing near Casimir warned.

"I know!" Lord Casimir grunted, slamming his fists on the dais railing. Throwing a Fae tantrum, he gnashed his teeth and scowled, but still said nothing.

"My lord!"

"Fine! I release the marriage contract on the grounds that you will have to renegotiate, Queen Maeve!"

An invisible weight lifted, causing Briar, the Queen, and Sawyer to take a breath.

"This isn't over, Maeve," Lord Casimir's voice carried a deadly threat.

Briar blinked, and Casimir was *gone*, along with his regiment of sniveling courtesans. All that remained was the settling of snow flurries spinning in the remnants of tornado-like funnels. Lord Casimir had whisked himself away, fuming at having to abandon his deal.

"Release him, Briar!" the queen cried.

"He's already doing it himself," Briar answered.

Silas broke the covering on his face by simply opening his jaw, causing it to crack. Licking his lips, he smiled at his girlfriend. "I always said you make the best ice-like creations with sugar."

"Sugar?!" Sawyer exclaimed.

"Yeah," Briar said, laughing. "I can't even make real ice, all of my magic is based on warmth, remember? It was just a trick."

Silas broke through the rest of the way, then leapt over the dais railing, jumping down to the lower floor. He didn't hesitate as he scooped Briar up, turning with her as he held her tight. "I can't believe you came all the way here, Briar. You might be crazy."

"Crazy about you. I had to help you, if I could. Wait ... you said my name!"

"Why wouldn't I?" he asked.

Briar shot a glance at the queen.

"I released your name already, you have proven yourself, proven your honor, and shown you are wise beyond measure. That you figured out to trick Lord Casimir ... it was brilliant."

Silas let Briar go, letting her talk to the queen more freely. Briar stepped closer to the dais, but the queen was the one to move within conversation range. She appeared directly in front of Briar, somehow instantaneously moving through space to stand with her, at her level. Not looking down on her from above, not from a place of judgment.

For the first time, she saw something in the queen's face: pride, and relief. "You gave me some clues. It was something you had said before," Briar said. "When I tried to melt your frozen heart, and you said "you can't melt what isn't there." But I realized what the truth was in that statement."

A soft smile tugged Queen Maeve's lips. "I'm glad you understood."

"Understood what?" Silas asked.

"It wasn't that her heart wasn't there, it was that *ice* wasn't there. Her heart wasn't frozen at all. A few things made me realize that she cared. She sends your dad supplies every season, no note, just makes sure he has what he needs. At any point I'm guessing she could have *made* him come back using whatever bargain is inked on his hand, like mine. Isn't that right, Sawyer? You have a Fae bargain tattoo hiding under that glove you always wear, don't you?"

Sawyer's jaw dropped. "Yes, I do." He slipped off the glove, revealing a matching design in dark blue ink of a star and snowflake design.

Briar nodded, not surprised that her hunch had been correct. "In addition to that, she sent Mirlah for me. At first I had thought you sent the will-o-the-wisp, Silas," she said, turning to him, "but then realized that it was probably the queen, and Mirlah was *helping* me. I remembered that it was her that assigned Mirlah to help you, and you probably couldn't change Mirlah's orders from the queen. If your mother really wanted you to go through with the marriage, she would have gotten rid of me. What could be worse for an impending arranged marriage than a girlfriend? Casimir might not have realized who I was to you when I was first here, but she did. She made the deal knowing it was you I was asking to bring back. And finally ....” Briar turned away from Silas to look at the queen again.

“Go on,” Queen Maeve urged.

“The way you looked when Silas came out to join us. Your facial expressions, though they were only for the smallest moment, I saw the worry in your eyes. I didn’t know what it meant exactly, but I thought you might not be able to stop what was happening.”

“You’re correct. I couldn’t do anything to negate the contract, I couldn’t even tell you or anyone how to get out of it, all I could do was leave little doors open and hope you found them. I have been trapped by this contract for longer than I have known you for, Sawyer. It existed as a first-born clause until Casimir chose to enact his intention when Silas was only four years old. I had hoped that Casimir would not pursue it, as Silas is half human, but that wasn’t the case. I have been bound by it ever since. When Silas wanted to escape Faerie to avoid the contract when he was older, I couldn’t even directly help him, but I did everything I could. When he was brought back, it was Casimir that had done it, not me.”

“Oh, Mother. I had no idea,” Silas said with a frown.

“I only wish your formative years were not marred by this,” the queen said.

“And now you’ll be forced to renegotiate,” Silas added.

Queen Maeve waved a hand. “It will be my problem to deal with, but it will be okay. I will make a deal with him to maintain our tenuous peace, *and* ensure you get the life you want to live. I needed out of that old bargain before I could open the path for you to do that."

"It will be *our* problem," Sawyer corrected. "I'll be here with you. I finally understand the things you couldn't tell me, and the heartache you carried because of it." He reached his ungloved hand toward the queen. She slipped her palm against his, and smiled.

The queen turned to Silas and Briar. "You two may return to Willowmere, and I suggest soon, as the Yule storm is about to commence. But I want you to know that you are welcome back any time, in fact I *want* you both to visit." She let go of Sawyer's hand, then opened her arms to invite a hug from Silas.

It took him a moment to realize, or maybe to process that his mother *actually* wanted to hug him. Given how he had barely spoken of her before they ended up waylaid in Faerie, Briar figured her showing him affection was not something that happened on a regular basis, if at all. Briar stood back as they awkwardly clasped in an embrace, clearly a little practice would be beneficial for a less weird experience next time. Still, her showing him that she loved him seemed to be welcomed by Silas. Briar thought she even spied a little glimmer of a tear in his eye. Who'd have guessed this little magically mixed family would evolve to get emotional?

Briar smiled at them both, beyond grateful that they were now on the other side of the drama, and in the end it had meant that healing could begin for them. Her eyes went wide as her thoughts snagged on *the other side*, the phrase reminding her of Tabby. She was still sitting in the in-between, waiting for Briar to come back. *Hex, she even warned me that Faerie makes you forget.* But, if she had been thinking about Tabby sitting in the shadow realm the whole time, Briar would have made choices out of panic.

But it did also mean it was definitely time to go.

"So, Briar Whittaker, is it? It's nice to finally meet you properly," Sawyer said as he gave Briar a hug. "Now make sure and come back to see us soon." Sawyer grabbed Silas for a hug next, the two of them making a lumberjack sandwich of manly, familial affection.

Queen Maeve raised her hands. "Enjoy your Yule celebration, and safe travels." A spiral of snowflakes surrounded them, blinding them for a moment. When it abated, they were at the portal, the entire trek from the castle cut short thanks to his dear ol' mom.

They smiled, one of those gut-punching, soft, hex-my-stars-I'm-in-trouble smiles. Briar tightened her grip on his hand, a dozen confessions bottlenecking in her throat. She'd love to stop here, kiss him stupid, maybe weep a little onto his coat which he looked very kissable in. But the Yule storm would stampede toward Willowmere at any moment and Tabby was still stuck in the damn shadow realm. Priorities. Romance was going to have to take a number. So instead, they shoved through the shimmering gate together, landing back in the seemingly sentient place where they started their relationship. Hollow Forest rustled in greeting like it remembered their drama.

Chapter 12

Tabby came hot-footing out of the shadow realm—literally—her pointy-toed boots smoking as she skidded to a stop, right as Briar and Silas arrived.

Briar snagged her in a fierce, breathless hug. "We've got to go. Yule storm is incoming, and it's about to pummel us sideways. Updates later."

Tabitha nodded, then looked at Silas. "Good to see you in one piece. Briar was *feral* before she went in to get you. Girl would not rest until she dragged you back home."

Briar blinked. She'd braced for a sassy welcome or a dramatic quip, but the relief softening Tabby's eyes was real.

"Glad to be back. Briar was amazing, you should have seen her." He squeezed Briar's hand, already pivoting toward the trees. "But we'll tell you everything once we're not about to die in a magical blizzard."

"As much as I know you want to hoof it through the forest, Moose, hedge riding is going to be our best bet."

"What? I can't hedge ride, that's … that's *insane*, Tabby!" he argued.

Instead of answering, she sliced a rift open like she was parting a curtain, stepping halfway through. She held both hands out. "Lucky for us, insane is kind of my brand. Let's go."

Briar took one of Tabby's hands, then flicked her eyes to the other waiting palm, wordlessly telling Silas to take it.

The portal shuddered violently behind them. A low groan rippled through the trees, followed by a roar like a wind turbine spooling up.

"Sounds like the forest just told you to get the fuck in," said Tabby.

Silas didn't hesitate. He grabbed her other hand and stepped in. "You don't have to tell me twice."

Briar had to imagine the narrow walk between worlds was a disconcerting, overwhelming experience for Silas, and the inability to speak was probably off-putting, but she also knew he could handle it. He had accompanied her that night back on Lughnasadh, helping her while she navigated the strange and terrifying deepest layers of the shadow realm. Silas had faced all of that beside her, and still hadn't run, he had shown he'd be steadfast by her side no matter what. The memory made her chest tighten in a way that had nothing to do with the liminal cold and everything to do with him. She tried glancing back at him as they wended between worlds, his silhouette blurring at the edges like ink in water. And of course, that was when she nearly snorted at herself.

Only she would get sentimental in the extradimensional equivalent of a haunted hallway.

They spilled out of a midair split right into the center of the village square. Dawn had only just cracked the sky, probably while they were trapped in the in-between, because it had still been night when they left the forest. Briar didn't have a second to breathe, much less process that she'd been awake all night *and* that everything she'd survived in Faerie had taken ... what, half a day?

Trudge through a magical realm, complete a queen-issued side quest, and rescue her boyfriend before Yule, all in under twelve hours? Please. Nothing a highly motivated witch with a pathological need to win a holiday countdown couldn't handle.

And now the Yule storm rolling in meant she was back just in time to finish her mountain of Yule cake orders. Good thing she actually loved baking, and had a few magical shortcuts up her sleeve to get those cakes across the finish line.

As much as she wanted to drag Silas behind closed doors and show him exactly how much she'd missed him, those orders came first. If she powered through them, she could close up shop early, grab her man, and disappear for the entire holiday. Yule Eve was go-time, customers would be lining up any minute to finish their own festivities.

"I've got to head to the shop to finish things up before the holiday. I know it's been a long night, so I'll see you both later."

Silas shook his head while Tabby chopped a hand through the air. "No way," Tabby said.

"Yeah, absolutely not," added Silas. "I'm coming to help."

"Me, too," her cousin said. "Let's get this done."

Briar sucked in a breath and smiled, tired, but ready for that second, wait .. third? Maybe fourth wind to pick up and carry her to completing this last task. "I'm lucky you both are as crazy as I am. Okay, let's do it!"

Bun Intended welcomed her back with its familiar warmth and smells of all of her past baked spells, the rich aromas saturated the space. She was light on her feet as she orchestrated the last of her Yule cakes creation, swishing her hands through the air as batter mixed, sugared decorations prepped, and pans baked. Briar admired her tattooed hand as she flicked her fingers toward the oven, the delicate designs inked into her skin now were a mark of acceptance and accomplishment. What had first felt like the visual stamp of obligation and risky agreements were now a sign of what she had been able to do in Faerie. The connection with Queen Maeve and the bridge formed between Silas and his family was an intangible Yule gift that she treasured above all else.

Tabitha and Silas both worked alongside her, helping shuttle completed cakes to the boxing area, packing everything up, complete with an evergreen sprig tied with a bow, and holly. It simply wasn't Yule without bringing a little of the forest inside.

It was during this baking bonanza that the storm finally hit, icing the whole area in a sparkling, otherworldly frost. The wind and white-out blizzard that had blown in with it were intense and powerful, but subsided in short order to reveal the town glazed in perfect icy grandeur. Briar smiled, it reminded her of the beauty of Queen Maeve's castle.

Before long, all orders were complete, with a steady stream of customers to pick up their ready-to-experience Yule magic. With the storm officially landed, it had heralded the flood of people that would descend on her tiny space. When the last one left the shop, Briar practically collapsed at her favorite table by the window. Silas and Tabby brought out coffee, and a tray of Briar's Joyful Gingerbread Cookies.

Briar didn't even need to bite into one in order to experience the cookie-induced bliss. All it took was one look at Silas, and she was home in her heart. She blew out a breath, the wave of everything that had happened crashed down upon her in an instant. It had been a mind-boggling night of adventures through a candy forest to face off with an ice queen, an ill-advised bargain with said ice queen *who turned out to be her boyfriend's mom*, tricking some Fae noble into releasing Silas from his bargain so she could whisk him home, and finally followed by a baking marathon to finish her very humble-by-comparison stack of seasonally spelled cake orders. Even with the coffee, exhaustion slammed her.

"I think our girl is cooked," Tabby mentioned over the rim of her mug. "Time to take her home, Moose."

Silas nodded. "Can we close up the shop, Briar? I think you've officially earned your holiday break."

Briar's eyes drooped, nodding. She was about two seconds from napping on the table right there. Fourth wind officially guttered out to nothing.

"I can take you both back by hedge riding," Tabby offered. "Unfortunately, I can't drive you, my car is at my house."

"No, that's okay, I have another idea," Silas said. He stood from the table, then headed to the back room to grab their coats, scarves, and of course his favorite satchel.

Wrapping her up in her jacket, he lifted Briar out of her chair, tucking her in close as he steadied her on her feet. "You know me, always one to hoof it through the woods," he said to both Briar and Tabby.

Briar looked up at him in question.

"Shortcut through Hollow Forest," he said to her with a half-smile. "Now that the storm arrived, we're good to take the path to your house. Nothing like returning to where it all started for us, except this time it's not you rushing headlong into the woods unaccompanied."

Briar grinned at him, thinking back on all the times since that night when the Hollow Forest had been their closest refuge for when they needed to quickly find an intimate spot. She nodded. "Hollow Forest it is."

As much as a shortcut through the forbidden path was … well, forbidden, she was anxious to get him home. And if anyone could make their way through the slightly spooky and sometimes dangerous route, it was Silas. "Want to come over in awhile to celebrate Yule Eve?" Briar asked Tabby.

Tabitha shook her head. "Nope, but thank you. I've got my date waiting for me." She waggled her phone in the air, indicating that she'd been messaging with the mystery man. "He waited for me all this time, I'm going to go give him his Yule gift."

"What?! Why didn't you tell me? All that time you helped me, he was *waiting for you?*"

Tabby winked. "Well, I may have indicated I'd give him an *extra special* gift. Because there was no way I wasn't going to come when you needed me." Tabby leaned over and pecked her cousin on the cheek. "And I'd do it again in a heartbeat."

"I owe you huge, Tabby. I love your guts."

"Yeah you do! Okay, I'm out of here. Yuletide Blessings, I hope you both have a much-deserved great time celebrating your escape from magical weirdo clutches."

Tabby slipped out through a rift, leaving Briar and Silas to head out after.

"What an exit!" Briar joked. "But I say we take the door."

Silas nodded and pushed the shop door open, swooping Briar up and carrying her through the village to the frost-covered tree line. The forest glimmered with the new fallen snow, Silas's boots crunched their way straight toward her little cottage on the east end of town.

Chapter 13

Being carried the whole way to her house was something Briar would have normally argued against. She was an independent woman, dammit. But being that close to Silas, and getting to catch a small rest while he walked them through a winter wonderland, was pretty swoon-worthy. As were the whiffs of his magic that bloomed off of him; they spurred delectable, toe-curling thoughts about what waited for her once they closed the door to her house. Fifth wind needed to arrive, stat.

Briar drifted off until the sound of his steps changed, the distinct wooden echo of her front porch stairs roused her. Flicking her fingers, she undid the magical lock to her front door.

The cold air swirled in with them, but the house welcomed them with warmth in spite of sitting dormant all night. Silas gently set her down on her feet, taking care to make sure she had her bearings before expecting her to be stable. She needed no such careful handling, as the moment she stood she turned toward him, catching his lips with hers while simultaneously swishing her hand behind him to motion the door closed. Another flick, and the door locked, ensuring they had all the privacy they needed.

Silas gripped her from behind as he kissed her, pulling her in as his scent magic kicked up. The smell of sueded petals, sparkling pine woods, and hearth-side embers swept the last of her exhaustion away.

Lessening the kiss, he lifted his head to look at her, the warm softening of his pupils as his eyes took in every detail of her face made her weak in the knees. The thought that he might not have been there, that he could have ended up trapped in Faerie with a future he didn't choose made her pause. Her heart thrummed with gratitude that they had been successful. They had *done* it. She had done it. She had not let doubt, fear, or anything else get in the way of getting him home. Because when he was with her, he was home, she could feel it in her heart.

Silas leaned down again, brushing his lips against her jaw and pulled her gently to guide her down the hallway toward the bedroom.

"Wait," she said, resisting the pull.

He stopped, the look on his face shifting from intrigue to worry. "What's wrong?"

"I ... *really* need a shower."

He laughed. "Hmm, you know, so do I."

She danced her fingers up his arms to his broad shoulders. "Then I think it would be wise if you joined me." Dirty girl wanted to get dirtier in that shower.

That was all the invitation he needed. In one motion he picked her back up, pulling her legs to wrap around his waist as he headed to the bathroom. By the time they were in the small space, she didn't have to concentrate on the spell to turn on the water; the thought of giving him her first Yule gift carried more than enough intention to set the water running. She was busier thinking about getting those clothes off of him.

They peeled off their layers, while trying to kiss at the same time, practically a magical feat in and of itself with the limited room they had.

The blessed hot water finally rained down on Briar, rinsing off the adventure, the worry, the stress, the preposterous nature of going there and back again through the strange, enchanted land of Faerie. She washed as fast as she could, anxious to get it over with so she could turn her attention back to Silas. Looking over at him, he washed with inhuman speed, his back muscles flexed as he turned away from her to make quick work of it. The thirst that rocketed to life as she saw the water bead up and run down over the curves and valleys of his skin made her bite her lip.

He swung his head and cocked one eyebrow at her, catching her staring. Turning to face her, his hardness was beyond evident as he reached for her, not waiting for any further sign. There was none needed, she was slick between her legs for him as he lifted her knee, then plunged himself into her. His strong hand pulling her from the hip while his other hand kept her knee aloft gave him plenty of leverage to angle himself expertly. The water splashed on them while he drew in stroke after stroke, and her head emptied out as they meshed together. Bakery orders, plans, worries, risky journeys, riskier Fae .. all of it left her mind as her whole existence tightened down to where they joined.

In an instant, he pulled out, then flipped her around, thrusting into her with a groan that made her tremble. His sounds, his smells, everything about him made her *want*. She couldn't get enough of him. Briar didn't care if it was magic, or something primal, or a blend of everything. All she knew was she never wanted him to stop. Silas's hands found her breasts, and light bloomed behind her eyes as release found her all too quickly. Pleasure detonated from her core, radiating outward in a blast which sent swells of sensation throughout her body. Silas had switched his grip to her hips, which tightened on her as he reached his apex of pleasure and unleashed an explosive moan.

Gasps of breath and rushing water was all she heard as they slowed, but she knew she instantly needed more. His cock still pulsed inside of her, the thick mass of it ebbing as he came down from the pinnacle they had reached. Separating herself, she moved to face him, kissing him while she let the water wash off the remnants of their joining. Briar didn't wait, though, she wanted more *now*.

Pulling him with her, she exited the shower and flicked her hand, turning the water back off. Briar barely gave time for a towel, before she led him into the bedroom, then guided him onto the bed so she could feel that magic that lived in him fill her from the inside.

With her legs folded on either side of him, his hard length leaped to life as Silas's eyes were on her naked, wet body above him. She sank down onto him, and the winter magic he had tried to hide previously came to life as well. Snowflakes dusted her skin, sending the smallest burst of cold that woke her up with a delighted shiver. The delicate flurries were gone before they barely touched her, melted away by the heat growing between Silas and Briar. It took Briar almost no time to return to that height of pleasure, her sex broadening against his and sending her into bliss. Nothing else existed in that state of euphoria, only she and him. They were all that mattered at that moment.

He sat up, his strong hand gripping the base of her head, pulling her hair a little to make her angle her chin up. Licking up the column of her neck, he then bit her at the joining of her neck and shoulder, right along the ridge of the prominent muscle that angled down. His canines pricking her sent a wave of pleasure through her, and the climax crashed in a stunning shockwave from what felt like the center of her very soul. Silas's whole body went taut at the same moment, his unleashing coinciding with her own.

Panting, and finally *officially* exhausted, she fell forward against him. The warm planes of his chest welcomed her, as he wrapped his arms around her. A skillful shift of his strong arms and he moved her to the side so she could lay her head on the pillow next to him. Silas pulled the soft, warm blankets around them, cocooning them as sweet sleep claimed her at last.

Midday into evening Yule Eve nap? Check. Wake up in the middle of the night for round three? Check. But this time, she needed closeness, she wanted a slower pace, a meeting of their souls along with their bodies, a celebration of their triumphs after trials. Either Silas was perceptive enough to read her cues, or he wanted the same measured pace after their first two breathless encounters.

Moonlight streamed in the window, rim lighting his handsome features as he braced himself above her. Briefly studying her face in the dim room, he lowered himself to kiss her with an aching reverence. The kind that told her she was who held his heart, his allegiance, his affection. It was always in his actions, the love that he held for her. As he backed off the kiss, he moved down the length of her, trailing his lips along every curve, until he reached her hips. Propping each leg over his shoulders, he swept back the narrow strip of hair above her clit, tugging it gently to reveal the glistening bud. The slightest smile turned up the corner of his lips as he opened his mouth and swept the soft tip of his tongue against her. The pulse that her body responded with made her back arch. Silas answered her movement with a satisfied groan and a longer lick up her center. That sound, it made her want to practically yell at him to fuck her immediately, but she was wholly reserved and instead pinched her eyebrows together as the intensity steadily increased. What admirable sexual restraint.

He continued with pass after pass, taking her to the edge until she pulled him up to meet her, insisting that he give her his hard cock at last. The gleam of his canine peaking out of a lazy, positively male smile caught her breath. Blue light painting the arch of his eyebrow, his straight, sculpted nose, and sharp jaw snagged her gaze. Every so often, his looks floored her. Most days it was his company she enjoyed, the way he made her smile or the way he showed how he felt about her. But on occasion that pure appreciation of his physicality took over and she was left reeling.

"You, in me. Right. Now," Briar demanded.

"Anything for you, my love." He reached down and grabbed his cock, then plowed into her.

She inhaled sharply, his sudden declaration stunned her, not to mention the steal-your-breath way his hard length stretched and filled her. Tears welled at her waterline, emotion threatened to make them spill. Briar's hands gripped his shoulders as she looked up at him.

"Shh," Silas said, moving in an ardent rhythm, pressing into her with each movement toward her. A kiss to her jaw, a kiss to her chest. His hand found the back of her head, and his thumb brushed her chin. "I love you, Briar. I should have told you ages ago."

Her eyes closed and she sobbed, the tears streaking back along her temples. "I love you more than anything, Silas. I couldn't bear to lose you."

He pressed his forehead to hers and let out a choking sound as he moved in and out again. She wrapped her hands around his low waist, pulling him into her harder with each thrust. He took a shuddering breath, watching their bodies come together, then pull apart only to return again. Scent magic swirled around them, the crackling embers and smoke at war with the blooming ice crystals. Silas snapped his gaze back up to hers, his eyes like glowing honey in the low light. He caught her lips and kissed her deeply, as he sped up the thrusts.

Her release was like dominoes falling. Spreading thought her body, her limbs, her toes, her whole existence. Her orgasm was the final descent of tumbling hopelessly in love. She had known she was well beforehand, she knew she would have never charged into Faerie the way that she did if she hadn't truly loved him, without a plan no less. But now? Now she owned that she was in love, it wasn't something that she would consider sidestepping and playing off as if it was "just dating." She knew she loved him long before she'd ever admitted it to herself.

He watched her fall, watched the surge of her nerves, the flood of emotions, and saw her final surrender to the madness. He fell with her, letting go with an unbridled roar.

Chapter 14

Dawn broke clean and clear. Briar stretched, feeling the location of the sun before she even opened her eyes. The solstice had a certain feel about it, she could *sense* that alignment of the sun, rising from its southernmost point and lowest arc across the sky. The day that marked the march toward spring, the promise of things to come. She rolled over to kiss Silas, only to open her eyes and discover he wasn't there.

Smells of cooking food and sounds of pans clinking from the kitchen made her grin. It was a good thing she loved him. Briar shook her head and laughed. The absolute audacity of that man to be *cooking* in a kitchen witch's hallowed space. Unheard of.

Pulling on her cozy, forest green fleece robe, she slipped her feet into the matching slippers, then shuffled out to inspect, no, *appreciate*, whatever he was making. Because whether it would have been considered cheeky or even crossing a line by other kitchen witches, Briar loved that he had taken it upon himself to fix them breakfast.

Greeted by French toast made with her own buttery-soft brioche bread, Briar's jaw dropped as she looked at the rest of the spread. Maple syrup that she wouldn't doubt Silas had probably extracted from the forest himself, poached eggs, pears stewed in cinnamon, fresh clementine wedges, and a side of sausage. Her eyes lit up as she not only saw the breakfast, but the man behind the work, wearing an apron and no shirt as he wielded a metal spatula.

"Excuse me, what is all this? You know how to make poached eggs?" she asked.

A wide grin split his face. "Surprise! The moose can cook! A little anyway, I don't often, but I thought I would for today." He untied the strings to remove the small canvas apron, not that it was covering much anyway, then motioned for her to sit at the counter so he could serve her.

"First things first, Merry Solstice, my love." She smiled at him, taking in the whole image again as she leaned over to give him a kiss. That man belonged on a Half-Fae Hot Male calendar. Maybe she'd ask for one next year.

"Happy Yule, my love."

Bright and beaming, the smile that spread on her face showed genuine joy. She sat down to finally take a bite. Looking around at the beautiful meal, she realized how grateful she was. In all honesty she had overlooked planning their Yule morning. She wasn't even a little prepared, she didn't even have a tree yet. It had to have been the first Yule that she didn't have a Yule tree, wreath, or pine swag up well before the big day. Getting any of those would have to wait, though, because for the moment she definitely needed sustenance.

It wasn't until she started eating that she realized how hungry she was. Coming back from Faerie in a rush only to get to her shop and bake her witchy little ass off, then back to her house to give Silas the welcome home he deserved, she realized they hadn't really eaten.

"You know, I have to admit," she said, motioning at Silas with her fork as she paused near the end of their meal, "I love seeing you with a spatula in your hand. I'd say it's as sexy as seeing you holding your axe. And that's saying something."

He laughed. "So you're saying you like watching me chop wood, too," he said as he poured her coffee he had freshly made.

Coffee. This man was going to make her clear the table with one arm and hop on him right there. She nodded at him as she cradled the cup, smiling at the thought.

"Well then, speaking of my lumberjack ways, if you're ready for a quick break ...." He nodded with his chin toward the living room.

Briar glanced to where he motioned, but there wasn't a clear view to the living room from where they sat. She took her steaming mug of coffee with her, then headed into the room.

The smell of fresh-cut pine nearly overwhelmed her. Silas had gone and cut down a tree, *and* brought in several pine boughs which he tied in a running swag over the window. Little white lights glimmered throughout, and brass ornaments of bells, globes, and crescent moons reflected the lights as they hung from the boughs.

The branches lifted slightly in greeting to her, acknowledging her skills as a green witch. She flicked her fingers, giving them all a little magical boost. With her daily blessing, she could keep the greenery in her house until the thaw came.

Sensing just how many branches he had brought in, she looked around the room in wonder at the amount of work he had clearly put in to make this Yule festive. Had she planned it, it would not have turned out nearly as wonderful. "You did this?! It's so beautiful, Silas!"

He nodded. "I noticed you didn't have a tree up yet, and figured with everything that had happened, you hadn't had time for it yet. I am a woodsman, after all, nothing a good axe swinging can't fix."

"You absolutely crazy amazing lumberjack maniac! How early did you get up?"

"Early," he admitted. "But you hadn't slept until last night, and I sort of had when I was in Faerie. When they darted me I was out for the entire passage from my house to Faerie, and then several hours after that."

"I'm sorry, *what*, that motherfucker *darted* you? If I ever see him again …"

"He did, I mean, they had to. I would have fought them the whole way. But, I made it out of Faerie in the end, all thanks to you." Silas took her in his arms again, threading his hands through the gaps made by her hands on her hips. "You're *amazing*, Briar. I'm convinced there's nothing you can't do. But it's also the way you do it. It isn't spiteful, or harmful. You navigate hard situations with grace. You've changed my life, you've even changed my father's *and* mother's lives."

Briar opened her mouth to respond, but no words came out.

"Here," he said, "I have something special for you."

Letting go to bend over and pick up a wrapped present under the tree, he handed it to Briar.

Roughly wrapped in plaid paper and tied with jute, the large package sat heavy in Briar's hands. She ran her fingers over it, smiling ruefully. "I'm so sorry, Silas, I don't have your gift yet. I meant to pick it up yesterday."

"You've already given me more than I could have hoped for," he said easily. "This is just something to show you how much I think about you when I'm not with you. Now open the damn thing!" He rubbed his hands together and bounced on his heels, utterly incapable of pretending he wasn't excited.

Her smile crinkled her eyes. He looked positively giddy as she settled the gift in her lap and tore away the paper. Inside was a beautiful bag, woven from fine reeds and grasses, preserved flowers stitched delicately into the design. She recognized the leather strap instantly, the same artisan's hand that had made his satchel. A running vine had been tooled into the leather, leaves and flowers curling along the stem. The perfect nod to her green witch heart that loved all things that grew.

"It's a basket bag," Silas said. "For picnics, or your bike rides to the shop. Or adventures you don't plan in advance." His mouth twitched with a slight smile. "And look inside."

She did, and blinked. A removable, washable liner, good for carrying pastries or ingredients she grew in her garden to add to her recipes. Beneath it, a smaller crossbody bag in the same woven style, complete with a matching floral leather strap. And beside that—

A canvas-covered album.

Her breath caught as she opened it. Photos of them, some moments she hadn't realized he'd captured. Laughing. Flour-dusted. That one rain-soaked day when they got drenched. All the small, ordinary magical moments of loving someone without noticing you were doing it. She swallowed hard and turned the pages until she reached the last photo. Several empty sleeves followed, and tucked into the plastic was a handwritten note.

For my beautiful Briar.
Whether the days are filled with adventure,
or spent busy at the shop,
I love spending them all with you.
I love you,
Silas

Click.

She looked up, startled, to find Silas lowering his phone. "Silas! I wasn't even ready!"

He laughed, then motioned for her to lean over to take a

picture with him in front of their tree, with the glimmering lights surrounding them. He kissed her cheek as he snapped the photo, and his magic unfurled without thought, snowflakes scattering around them, light and effortless. When they looked at the picture together, the moment was perfectly framed: unplanned, unscripted, and exactly right.

Briar leaned into him, heart full, thinking that maybe Sawyer had been right all along.

Adventure really did start where plans ended.

THE END

Acknowledgments

First and foremost, a huge thank you to my readers. I appreciate each and every one of you for your time. The fact that you are now here, reading my acknowledgments at the end of this book means you have spent your time reading it, and I am so grateful that you did. It's because of my readers that I am here at this point, able to thank you because this book marks my tenth release. Ten books! There's no way I would be here if I didn't have you along with me on this journey. So a heartfelt thanks goes to you. I'm excited to share more books with you and to bring you more great stories to spend your cozy time with.

Thanks go out to my husband, Kirt, and our three kids. You all are the light of my life and prove to me that magic is real. I'm honored to be a part of your lives and to live each day with you.

To my best friend and fellow wordsmith, Laura L. Hohman. To all of our adventures, both writerly and in real life, thank you for all of them!

Thank you to my friends and family that have supported me on this adventure, who have offered their words of encouragement and/or told me of their pride in me. That means a lot to me and I'm very grateful to have people close to me that have my back.

To my friend, Josefine Fouarge, who runs the Youtube channel Fine Reads, and who shows the indie author community consistent support in so many ways. For what you do for the community, and for the support you have shown me, a huge and emphatic THANK YOU! Now to everyone reading this, go subscribe to her Youtube channel and get great reading recs!

To my friends and fellow authors on BookTok, I'm proud of our community and glad for the support we all offer each other. I can honestly say I've made real friendships and connections there, and believe that my author journey is that much better and more fulfilling because of our ability to lift each other up.

To all of the practitioners that bring peace and light to this world (and maybe a few well-deserved hexes) I tip my pointy hat to you, sisters and brothers, for harnessing the divine feminine and for strengthening the magic that surrounds us.

About the Author

Raised in a rural town called Elfin Forest, magic and inspiration surrounded Lorin throughout her childhood. A mile down the road from her small town was the equally magical town of Harmony Grove, where the witches and psychics lived. Having such neighbors inspired her with wonder early on. Fantastical stories permeated her life, and eventually she started writing her own. An award-winning fantasy and science fiction author, Lorin loves weaving epic tales that retain human-relatable experiences with a kernel of truth. She believes the vastness of the human spirit can be explored through fiction, and through it we can discover more about ourselves. Lorin can always be found with a book nearby, absorbing stories or crafting her own. She lives in Southern California with her husband and three kids, loves nature, and is always doing something creative.

Thank you for reading! If you enjoyed this book I'd be very grateful if you posted a short review. Your support really makes a difference, leaving a review is one of the most impactful things you can do for an author. Thank you for your support!

Get updates on release information, exclusive giveaways, and insider info by signing up for my newsletter at www.lorinpetrazilka.com

Other Books by Lorin:
Harvest Magic and Other Poor Decisions - book 1 in the Witches of Willowmere series
Samhain Eve Masquerade

Vale Born - Vale Born series book 1
Plight of the Syrenni - Vale Born book 1.5
Pull of the Vale - Vale Born book 2
Yoke of the Vale - Vale Born book 3
Vale Born: The Complete Series
Song of Blood and Mist

The Zenith Decoy
co-written by Lorin Petrazilka and Laura L. Hohman
Not So Silent Nights: A Collection of 3 Holiday Novellas
co-written by Lorin Petrazilka and Laura. L. Hohman

www.ingramcontent.com/pod-product-compliance
Lightning Source LLC
Chambersburg PA
CBHW030542130626
46552CB00006B/2374